# Strange
# Growth

Niko Kristic

# CONTENTS

# ACKNOWLEDGMENTS

With everlasting gratitude to all the friends who offered valuable advice (and tolerated my company) during the composition of these tales…

# POLITENESS

Professor Percival Quilloughby sat in the carriage with his briefcase on his knees like a far-fetched, dear-bought, deeply mistrusted and generally reprehensible dog. The train was whiffling by at a sightseer's tempo, and like a sightseer was stopping and starting at much too regular irregular intervals. This gave the professor ample opportunity to scrutinise its numerous indiscretions, along with those of his briefcase, the weather, the drowsing lout a few seats across, and invariably himself. To begin with, the briefcase – containing his notes, his collapsible travel-umbrella, an ecclesiastic-historical volume of reference, and the perfectly triagonal cheese sandwiches which were his constant and only fare – threatened to upend itself with every lurch and jolt of the train. Matters were not helped by its precarious situation on the summit of his kneecaps. A lesser man might have been tempted to colonise the empty seat adjacent, but to the professor such a thing was unthinkable. How could he forgive himself for depriving some theoretical future passenger of its inviting and perfectly functional berth? Of course, established protocol dictated the employment of those overhead storage racks with which modern carriages like this one were amply and generously equipped. But to Professor Quilloughby's profound consternation, the drowsing churl's mangled old guitar-case – slung up as carelessly as a corn-sack in the barn-rafters – was *invading* the space which rightfully corresponded to *his* row of seats. A lesser man, no doubt, would have forsaken his principles and violated the sanctuary of his neighbour's overhead storage. But to *trespass* with such *flagrant lawlessness* on another's theoretical property – however impermanent, implicit, and unlikely to be occupied – was an act so abominable that it turned the sensitive cheddar lining of the professor's stomach. How could anyone possibly inflict such impropriety on an innocent stranger? The very hypothetical was enough to ruin his day.

The train jolted and the churl snorted himself awake. Professor Quilloughby averted his eyes in horror but continued watching the gruesome spectacle unfolding in the window. The churl yawned through yellow tusks, his breath fogging up the glass already smeared in sleep with the oily secretions of his forehead. He raised a hand – an appreciable effort, thought the professor, but alas, too little too late – before permitting himself a little gasp of shock when the man's vile trotter came down instead to scratch at a stubbly jowl. The man yawned again. *God grant me distraction,* thought the professor. He shifted fractionally in his seat. He could not peel his eyes from the itching, grunting, slobbering lump that was the reflection of the creature across from him. What was he doing now? Was *that* – no. It couldn't be. It was in excess of all conceivable reality. Small whimpering sounds inadvertently escaped the professor's throat as the scofflaw clumsily pinched tobacco into a rolling-paper. The carriage passed over a join in the rails and the filter flew from his fingers with a distinctly audible curse. The professor winced. He fumbled for another. The *NO SMOKING PLEASE* sign blazed directly over the villain's fat cobloaf head. The professor began to feel queasy as the carriage filled with imaginary smoke. His suitcase fell over and, in light of more pressing issues, was righted without complaint. Outside, raindrops like tiny pearlescent molluscs were beginning to leave trails on the window-glass; were breaking their surface-tension shells on the leaves as though dropped by a great crow stirring storms with its wingbeats – when salvation hove into view. His prayers had been heard. Nantwich station. Wrenbury was only a stop away – but with any luck, this would be the end of the journey for the churl. The carriage rolled to a halt by the platform. The churl began to roll another cigarette. Professor Quilloughby nearly keeled over. A lesser man, of course, would have cut his losses and bolted for the platform; a bracing five-mile hike to Wrenbury in the rain was, as prospects went, not entirely unappealing. But there was no way to do it without offending, or at least disconcerting, the only other passenger in the carriage – swinish brute though he was. To bustle from the train like a pheasant beaten out of tall grass could be seen as nothing other than an evasive manoeuvre, which was always improper in peacetime among civilians. And though every fibre of his being yearned to respectfully educate the young gentleman about his contravention of the common social rubric, the professor was held back by his stomach, which, of all his bodily apparatus, was most sorely deficient in fibre of any kind. For five miles he held his breath and watched the cigarette smouldering on the stranger's smile like a herpetic sore.

One might be forgiven for the omission of Wrenbury station on the transport map. It was unmanned save for a faunish tomcat recumbent as a woodsprite among shadows of ivy, sheltering from the rain whose uneven sobs were now threatening to cascade. The professor unfurled his telescopic umbrella. At least the rain would help to exorcise the acrid whiff of tobacco that possessed his imagination and therefore his tweeds. On that note, he redid the upper two buttons of his jacket (for it was proper etiquette to unfasten them while seated), and nervously prayed he should not encounter another umbrella-bearing walker heading the opposite direction. No etiquette had yet been developed to account for this situation, and as such the professor considered it a socially innavigable nightmare to be avoided at all costs. Worrying thus he left for the village, nearly stepping on the stationmaster who simply yawned and relaxed his sylvan length to the hypnotic percussion of water on leaves.

Professor Quilloughby had never before found it necessary to indulge in something quite so irregular as a research trip. As an undergraduate he had set foot in the University library and, whether for reasons of convenience or anxiety, never quite set foot out of it. But today was different. Like a penitent he had braved the locomotive pilgrimage to Cheshire, suffering changeovers more convoluted than the circulatory system of a conjoined twin, in pursuit of edification both academic and profoundly personal. For professor Quilloughby was the first man in centuries to seek after *Politeness*, who knew where to find it. Here some clarification may be advantageous. The name 'Politeness' is given by scholars to a lost poem in the English alliterative tradition, dating to the early fourteenth (or perhaps late thirteenth) century, ascribed to the mysterious and heretofore unidentified Gawain poet. Some details of its matter have been reconstructed from Sir Robert Cotton's (sadly fragmentary) eighteenth century commentary, supplemented by the scholarship of mediaevalists in the French romance cycles, which appear to have contained some possible narrative analogues. *Politeness* seems to have been the story of Sir Ormerod (perhaps to be identified with Sir Esmeragde of the extant romances), a knight sworn to uphold the poem's eponymous virtue. During the course of the poem, Sir Ormerod progresses through a gauntlet of trials, the exact nature of which is sadly lost, but against which he persistently triumphs with the aid of noble courtesy and graciousness. That is until his final challenge: a boar-hunt, which Ormerod (true to his nature) insists on treating as a courtly tilt. Of course, the beast, unconstrained by the conventions of civility, swiftly spells the knight's doom. The poem is believed to have concluded with an extended passage of didactic or possibly homiletic nature, most likely treating themes of moderation and the perils of surquedry in virtue. While *Politeness'* dearth of scribal transmission suggests that it did not enjoy any significant popularity in the Middle Ages (doubtless on account of the poet's rather archaistic north-west midlands dialect), its value to modern scholarship would be utterly priceless. For as professor Quilloughby himself had extensively argued, *Politeness* almost certainly represented a dry-run of surviving Middle English romance's crowning glory, *Sir Gawain and the Green Knight.* Indeed, much of the otherwise conjectural evidence for *Politeness'* ascription to the same authorial source derives from similarities noted by Cotton to the third fitt of *Sir Gawain.* The specialist lexicon and exquisite pacing of the latter poem's boar hunting set-piece suggested a reworking of Sir Ormerod's climactic duel, with further strong evidence to suggest that Sir Gawain's infamous betrayal of chivalric virtue was essentially a more nuanced and mature poetic treatment of Sir Ormerod's original lapse of judgement. Professor Quilloughby further suspected that the envoy of *Politeness* constituted a missing link between the poet's work in the romance tradition and their didacticism in the extant though more generically ambiguous *Cleanness* and *Patience.*

Yet it was one of the great tragedies of mediaeval scholarship that all such conclusions were necessarily speculative, for the only known copy of *Politeness* perished in the Ashburnham House fire which claimed so many priceless manuscripts in 1731. The only evidence that the poem had ever existed in the first place was its description in the Cottonian library archival catalogue, of which fragments survived the blaze. I pray you will permit this brief diversion into the dynamic world of textual history; indeed it is crucial to understanding the more-than-merely quixotic character of professor Quilloughby's quest. After the Dissolution of the Monasteries under King Henry VIII, many ancient manuscripts that had once belonged to monastic libraries were scattered around the country, finding themselves in the possession of independent owners often ignorant of their cultural value. It was the supreme talent of Sir Robert Cotton, one of the first and greatest members of the Society for Antiquaries, to identify and procure these diasporic artefacts – among which, for instance, was the original *Gawain* manuscript, *Cotton Nero A.x* – assembling a collection that would eventually form the foundation of the British Library. Following Sir Robert's path through Cheshire in an earlier period of research, professor Quilloughby – who had been hunting after the geographical origins of the *Gawain* MS – had quite accidentally discovered the probable first location of the *Politeness* holotype.

Combermere Abbey was once a Cistercian monastery, coincidentally acquired and rebuilt into a country house after the Dissolution by one Sir George Cotton; no relation to the famous antiquary who visited to empty its vaults of remaining textual treasures several centuries later. It is believed that *Politeness*, which manorial records suggested that Sir Robert had procured from the estate in the early 1720s, had been part of the original monastic library obtained by Sir George with the Abbey itself – whose own peculiar history formed the crux of professor Quilloughby's present intuition. Combermere Abbey was considered dissolute long before its forcible Dissolution; indeed its reputation for debauchery was well-recorded. Rather less well-recorded however were the actions of a small but highly devoted group of monks, evidently (and as the professor thought, quite rightly) disgusted by the Abbey's abyssal standards of morality, who formed a renegade sect and abandoned Combermere to occupy a small friary in the village of Wrenbury. Quite likely they avoided further persecution through masquerading as secular clergy. This little known and still less remarked-upon historical curiosity was important to the professor for a single reason, since these recreant monks were thought to have made copies of a large number of Combermere's monastic texts to populate their own fledgling library – copies so far uncatalogued and unstudied. It was probable, indeed, it was more than likely, that a second copy of *Politeness* would be found among them. And it was just such a copy that professor Quilloughby sought upon this rainy and already much-too-eventful afternoon.

Wrenbury in the rain was as drowsy as its stationmaster, and following a gentle bend of the river Weaver to its centre professor Quilloughby had the good fortune not to encounter a single umbrella'd pilgrim to compromise his brittle self-assurance on the narrow track. The welcoming old-worldliness of St. Mary's chapel caught his eye immediately – the small though lovely church-like edifice adjoining could be nothing other than the friary. Yet as the professor drew closer, he could see that its loveliness, and indeed that of the chapel, was rather of the tragic order. Stone as friable as the pages of an old quire, statuary as smooth-worn as speleothems, arches skewed sideways in the shape of slipped ribs: a moribund beauty, like the lucid last minute of a much-beloved relation. Indeed its condition was only a few shades away from the carrion architecture of old Combermere Abbey, whose ruins still stood, defying chronology, on the country house grounds. An ugly old gentleman of the quintessential English (and thus, to the professor, honest and reliably approachable) phenotype was sheltering under the chapel eave with a tin mug of steam. Presumably he was the chapel verger, or, in preferable archaism, its sacristan. Drawing closer, professor Quilloughby cleared his throat with a squeak seldom heard outside arguments in the creole of damp rags and dirty windows. He was always cautious of interrupting people; the risk of committing indiscretion or even *faux pas* was usually much too severe, but in this rare edge-case, as a stranger in a new village, the professor was quite confident of his conversational right-of-way.

'Excuse me sir, hullo, yes – could you please tell me where I might find St. Mary's chapel?' The man regarded him with the studied disinterest of a Kantian aesthete. 'You're lookin' at it, sir', he said, sucking steam. 'Am I? Of course, thank you, ha ha ha – silly me'. Optimising the cohesion of the social encounter, professor Quilloughby toggled his register a few increments towards its rather dusty and under-utilised 'demotic' setting. 'Could I maybe have a look inside? Would love to pop into the friary too if, err, if that's good by you. I'm a scholar you see, sir, very interested to talk to the monks. I mean, the friars'. 'No can do, sir'. 'Beg your pardon?' 'No can do. "Heritage at risk" site, sir, grade two. I tend the grounds, no visitors allowed'. 'But what about the m-the friars?' 'Sir you're a clever man with a fancy umbrella but I'm afraid there ain't been any friars 'ere for nigh-on a hundred years. Just shadows and stones, and a bit of ivy on Christmas when I'm on holiday'. 'Erm, right. Thank you. I mean – a hundred years, you say? What happened to them? I was very much hoping to visit their library'. Another slurp of steam. 'Oh, you can still do that, sir. Just not here. Hundred years back Lord Combermere made a fuss about St. Mary's, as part of the Abbey it was his land by rights, but the friars were still usin' it. It *is* part of my job to know this stuff, sir. Eventually they shoved off and made their own little church out in the forest, no-one goes there but them, really. It's very, what's the word, exclusive. Reclusive'. 'And there are still people living there?' 'Course there is. You see 'em about the place, now and then, come into the village market. Church is an hours' walk south from here, follow the path and you won't miss it'. Still reeling in the aftermath of having trusted the accuracy of so outdated an ecclesiastical Baedeker, professor Quilloughby offered the verger his slightly too profuse, slightly too sincere thanks. 'Stay out of trouble', the old man said, and watched the animate suit-briefcase-umbrella recede into the rain. He'd tell his daughter he'd seen another ghost.

Professor Quilloughby held his chin high as he broke into the forest. He had been marginally misinformed, that was true, but had come out of the conversation with his dignity unscathed, and his prize still well within reach. Water off a telescopic travel umbrella's back. At some point he noticed a trailside bench, and, accurately predicting the dwindling frequency of such opportunities, patted it dry to enjoy his crustless triangles of cheddar and wholegrain. Dainty nibbles and handkerchief corners affronted the wilderness, and the weather did not seem disposed for mercy by the time professor Quilloughby continued his descent into the forest. Twists of ilex wyrmed darkly about the low trunks of thickening trees, their crowns shaking in the wind like a council of giants in solemn disagreement. The dirt path, seldom provoked, clung noisomely to the professor's shoes; the low growth of brambles and deceptively unpliable ferns snagged on his wet-sheep jacket. This was a place for wodwos and waerlogas. This path was trod only by wild beasts and itinerant thunders. And it was certainly longer than an hour's walk before professor Quilloughby arrived at the friary. In the fading light it was actually a rather impressive sight. Part of him had expected an archipelago of rustic hovels, a clerical shanty-town cut off from good sense and civilisation – but here was a building as comely as St. Mary's, if slightly less elaborate, slightly more overgrown – and indeed, figured the professor with curiosity, slightly more ancient. He certainly did not recall reading of such a thing around the Wrenbury environs in his well-thumbed volume of reference. Light glowed from its narrow windows. Professor Quilloughby disciplined his tie, and, eager to escape the elements, squeaked his throat clean before greeting the heavy oaken door with a well-mannered rap of the knuckles. No response but the grumbling of the wind, the hiss and rattle of the rain through holly. Begrudgingly he raised the great iron knocker – usually much too forceful an announcement for his tastes – and flinched as it dropped. Suddenly his tiny corner of forest grew cosy with firelight as a burly man in a dark green habit appeared at the door.

'Come in, come in!' he beckoned, face rosy with welcome. Professor Quilloughby gave a decorous smile and fumbled to retract the umbrella whose spread was just too large to fit through the doorframe. His smile wavered as he felt the fellow's strong hands pull him into an embrace, then inverted to ill-concealed revulsion as the man's great beaver-coloured beard brushed his cheeks in a decidedly continental greeting. Professor Quilloughby turned red. At least amongst his older peers in the Faculty, francophobia was second cousin to courtesy – but something told him that here wasn't quite the place. His upper lip recalibrated into genial stiffness. 'Welcome to our humble Abbey,' said the man, 'I am brother Marcel. You must let me take your suitcase – the umbrella you shall bring along with us to dry by the fire'. Professor Quilloughby was still processing the situation. 'Charmed', he began, 'thank you ever so much. I'm professor-' The man interrupted with jolly grace. 'Not until you've broken bread with us by the fire, stranger. The laws of hospitality demand it! Come, let me show you our humble hall'. The professor followed the monk into a stone-walled chamber that flickered with the light of a blazing hearth, gilding the fierce tusks of the boar's head mounted on a shield above. The walls were draped with plain hangings of pleasing archaism, and several monks, who had been seated in low chatter at the long table on the dais, stood up to greet the newcomer. Professor Quilloughby received and, to his bewilderment, somehow *bestowed* more kisses in that minute than in the preceding lifetime. 'The others are preparing supper, for which you will join us' explained brother Marcel, mantling a chair with the professor's tweed jacket and transporting it to the fireside. Very soon, attended by the ministrations of brother Marcel, brother Tobias and brother Hubert, the professor was dry and comfortable, though it would severely understate the extent of his neuroses to imply that Percival Quilloughby could ever be truly 'at ease'. 'I've been studying the ecclesiastical history of this area for a long time, but I never knew that such a place as this, err, your Abbey even existed'. 'Yes, it's not very well known, and you're quite fortunate to have stumbled upon it all the way out here. It was a small alien priory, under Norman jurisdiction, before the Dissolution – though it managed to survive, I believe, through reversion to extreme insularity. As the story goes there were only two elderly monks lingering on by the time our forefathers arrived from their exile and assimilated here. But enough of this, my friend. As the werewolf Gorlagon said unto Arthur: "dismount and feast and rest today, because I see that you are weary from the stress of the journey, and tomorrow I will tell you what I know"'. Brother Marcel gave a ruddy grin. The monk was citing mediaeval literature? In such unexpectedly familiar territory, the professor found courtesy effortless. 'Is that your own translation? You are learned men, I see!' 'We are blessed with a fine library', smiled brother Tobias, when two other green-robed figures entered, bearing platters, bowls, and cutlery for the service of the evening meal.

Professor Quilloughby, peckish in spite of his sandwiches, graciously accepted the offer of hospitality – though not without a twinge of misgiving. He did not wish to appear ingratiating, not in the least, but while he was under the roof of such a company, *especially* a company from which he had something very tangible to gain – it would only be civil to respect and partake in their customs. Therein lied the nature of this misgiving. These monks – as he had been so rudely informed at the door – spoke a very different dialect of politeness. Inside their Abbey, the boundaries of courtesy shifted. Professor Quilloughby knew he would have to shift with them, or – to his unimaginable chagrin – he would appear socially illiterate, ignorant, even uncouth. The next mortification came with the dining arrangements. 'Our guest shall be my dining partner', said brother Marcel, gesturing widely to one of three places set on the long table. There were six men in the hall. Professor Quilloughby smiled weakly. Grace was intoned in a language like the Latin of educated Normans, and the professor's spirit wilted further when the first course – some ghastly pottage in a shallow wooden bowl – was ladled out between them. As a rule, professor Quilloughby followed a highly restricted diet. In childhood his mother had once mentioned the fact of his sensitive digestion and he had believed her ever since. But he had been through the gauntlet of school dinners, where the gruel could not have been less gruelling than this, and so he dipped his spoon and gave a delicate slurp. Dishwater with onions. Brother Marcel's beard was damp with it, and, thanks to the professor's unfamiliarity with dining-partner etiquette and lack of coordination – so was his sleeve:

'I'm dreadfully sorry'. The monk used the same sleeve to wipe his beard, then feigned surprise at the state of it. 'Silly me', he winked, and the table laughed aloud while the professor produced some counterfeit equivalent. A mess of pottage, he thought darkly, a pot of message. Brother Hugo poured wine from a large jug into six silver goblets. The professor, obviously a lifelong teetotaller, accepted his cup with what he thought was an air of cultivation, and, following the example of the other monks, clashed it with that of his partner. It tasted like ink and vinegar, but he drank despite his throat's best efforts to turn the tide.

Brother Hugo and brother Estienne had gone to fetch the next course, and the others fell to talking. Professor Quilloughby introduced himself and where he had come from. His speech was slower than usual, which was disconcerting, and the room was growing warmer. The glassy eyes of the mounted boar, enormous and bristlier even than brother Marcel, silently judged him as he spoke. 'In all, gentleman, I have come to ask a great favour – that I might be allowed, err, with permission, to look at your library – and hopefully find a lost copy of *Politeness*'. There were approving murmurs from the monks. 'I've read it', said brother Hubert. 'Me too, actually' remembered brother Tobias, 'it's quite good'. Professor Quilloughby's heart began to hammer. 'S-so you have, err, have a copy?' Brother Marcel laughed thunderously. 'Oh yes, we have it! It's probably our most valuable document'. 'You're most welcome to read it, of course', interjected brother Tobias, 'provided you follow the correct rules and rituals'. 'But of course-' stammered the professor, 'I wouldn't dream of violating-' 'And that's not all we have, is it brothers?' resumed Marcel, who the professor increasingly suspected was slightly hard of hearing, 'of course, professor, you were not aware – but there's a reason this little Abbey of ours was built in such an obscure spot in the forest, so long ago'. 'The holy site', nodded brother Hubert, sipping wine, 'Sir Ormerod's tomb'. 'Sir Ormerod's tomb?' repeated the professor, slightly louder than he strictly intended. The world was starting to waver. His was the only empty cup. 'Oh yes, down in the undercroft, where we also keep *Politeness*'. 'C-Can I see it?' 'Steady, professor! We're quite sure it'll still be there tomorrow morning. For now let us eat, make merry and rest'. Brother Marcel addressed him with a twinkle in his eye. 'And what's your fascination with *Politeness* anyway, my friend?' The professor started, vision darting. 'Well, err, it's a bit like chivalry, isn't it? An elite, err, social language, that we speak by performing... so that everything runs smoothly'. Brother Marcel smiled. 'I meant the poem'. The only performative language Professor Quilloughby could muster was perspiration. 'Right, my apologies – of course'. And as if by omnipotence of thought, brothers Estienne and Hugo arrived with the next course. Three huge golden trout on a riverbed of strange green vegetation stared up from three silver dishes, doused in some pungent potion whose culinary application struck the reeling professor as dubious at best. 'Fresh from the Weaver', said brother Hugo, as the others gave their earnest thanks. 'Can I, err, see the poem tomorrow morning, then?' asked professor Quilloughby, faintly. His dining partner put a reassuring hand on his shoulders. 'I will personally see to it that you do, my friend. You have my honest word'.

\*\*\*

Professor Quilloughby did not want to remember the night that had followed supper with the monks. Their bizarre little Abbey in the forest was not large enough to have an open cloister, and so its inhabitants slept in their own little chambers. But to combat the 'immorality' that such arrangements had historically fostered at Combermere, it was customary for each monk to lie with a bedfellow. And as brother Francis was away on some religious duty, it had fallen to the professor to uphold that custom. Brother Marcel had generously offered his company, but after a quite excruciating interchange the professor had joined the rather quiet and elderly brother Estienne instead. After an evening service they had gone up to their chambers, and professor Quilloughby had done whatever lies in between brewing a terrible headache and pretending to sleep. Brother Estienne had risen with the dawn to perform some devotional obligation which guests were mercifully not expected to attend, giving the professor a chance to snatch a few starveling and solitary hours of slumber from the jaws of defeat. Unfortunately, this only seemed to give his headache a renewed opportunity to incubate, and by the time he awoke the professor felt thoroughly wretched and wearier than before. The clothes he had folded over the chair with a geometer's exactitude had been replaced with a fresh robe of forest green. Was there anything more distressing, he thought, than having to wear someone else's clothes? His mind swung back to the sleeping arrangements. Whimpering quietly, he accepted his sartorial destiny – to do otherwise, of course, would be tantamount to insolence.

Professor Quilloughby timidly made his way downstairs to the main hall. Brother Marcel was waiting for him there. 'Good morning, brother Percival!' he said, splitting his face with a grin. 'Ah, erm, yes, quite' said the professor, thinking better of it, 'good morning brother Marcel'. 'You're just in time to join me for some breakfast. Don't you worry, I haven't forgotten my promise. The others are making preparations down in the undercroft. There are some funny old conventions we have when a guest asks to see *Politeness*, you see – given the location of our sanctuary, it's almost a holy book for us. That hardly ever happens, of course, so I must tell you we're all rather excited. Nothing to be worried about, professor! Just a bit of harmless fun, I do hope you'll play along'. The professor's head throbbed. 'Thank you, brother Marcel'. Breakfast awaited him on the table – breadsops in spiced wine. His head throbbed harder. It would be impolite to refuse. The hall looked strange in the young light of morning. Somehow smaller, more austere, almost spare, nowhere near as high and fantastical without the glamour of rain lashing outside, without logs crackling in the fire, without, without... something else was missing, but the professor couldn't quite put his finger on what. The wine was robbing him of his wits, and his stomach was beginning to roil. He half-expected the burly monk at any moment to inquire how he'd slept, but to the professor's blessed relief that particular question appeared to be outlawed in both their idioms of courtesy. Although he wasn't sure why this was a concern. Brother Marcel had so far treated him only with perfect kindness – of a kind, yes, a foreign kind, but kindness nonetheless. And he was quite sure that all his reservations would dissolve the moment he laid eyes upon his holy grail: the *Politeness* manuscript. The monk's chair scraped on the stone dais as he rose, patting his belly with a sigh of contentment. He smiled through his great rusty beard. 'Now if you're quite ready professor, please do follow me'.

Brother Marcel had to bow his head to clear the low stone archway of the staircase leading down to the undercroft. 'On your left is the wine-cellar, you know, the monks who lived here before our brotherhood used it for a reclusion-chamber... but they were very severe. Much stricter than us! Yes, here we are. Mind your step'. Professor Quilloughby couldn't quite tell if the monk's inane ramblings were a comfort or an irritation. For the longest time he had imagined this moment as a quiet *eureka* alone in some dusty library, but if these monks insisted on a bit of pomp and ceremony about it all, it wasn't his place to complain. He was bound by broken bread and honour to be as civil and inoffensive as humanely possible, and that meant following the great unspoken laws to the tee – especially their idiosyncratic local varieties. The undercroft was a subterraneous chamber, nearly as large as the dining hall, illuminated by candles flickering from cobbled alcoves. Four great pillars, one in each corner, supported the vaulted roof, and around these clustered brothers Hubert, Tobias, Estienne and Hugo all with smiles of expectation on their candlelit faces. Professor Quilloughby felt fresh straw crinkling under his beslippered feet. The whole place smelled of straw and wax and stone and some leathery musk which the professor could not immediately identify but probably arose from an event horizon of unwashed men in an unventilated space, if not from ancientness itself. Now his own expression lit up with delight and expectation. Facing him in the centre of the room was a carven lectern, atop which lay dormant a quarto so utterly ancient-looking that one was almost surprised to note that evolution had afforded it a vertebral column – but indeed, the tome's spine was magnificently ribbed and gilded and chained to the lectern where it rested. It could contain nothing other, thought Professor Quilloughby, than the *Politeness* manuscript.

But that was not all that attracted his antiquarian eye – nor indeed, perversely, the item which magnetised it most strongly. For positioned sideways in front of the lectern was a colossal stone sarcophagus. Its lid was decorated in high relief with the sculpture of a supine warrior, whose gauntleted stone hands rested on the pommel of an antique broadsword glittering through the ambient murk. Even in the low candlelight, the professor could discern a few words from the Latin legend on its base:

*SIR ORMEROD*. It was more than he had ever dreamed of. He momentarily felt the warmth of brother Marcel's powerful hand on his shoulder. 'You'll know what to do, professor', he whispered with a wink, striding past to assume his position by the lectern. His big voice boomed through the stony chamber. 'Be welcome, brother Percival, to the holy undercroft of our Abbey. Let the ceremony begin!'

Professor Quilloughby heard shuffling from the pillars behind him – and suddenly couldn't breathe. He couldn't see. He started to struggle but his voice wouldn't work. It was as if some great ungainly bag had been pulled over his head – but he *could* smell. It reeked of rancid leather with an aftertaste of turpentine, uncannily like a badly restored and putrescent vellum. 'Get it off me, get off!' he cried, but where language should have spilled was only the acid bilge of spiced wine rising in his gullet. He felt leather thongs tightening around his upper arms, intense weight pushing down on his head, and then he felt the monks let go of him and step away, laughing merrily. 'Please!' he begged, 'please!', but his pinioned limbs could not remove the obscene and stinking device. 'One moment!' he heard the chortling voice of brother Tobias, and a dull thump on the back of his head. Suddenly the professor could see again, though only through the narrowest of visors – a visor rimmed with the wickedly pronged tusks of an enormous wild boar. He let out a scream of horror and rage. The monks clapped their hands and laughed with unconstrained mirth. 'It's just a game, professor!' they called, 'don't worry, just play along!' But some tiny shrunken part of professor Quilloughby already knew the rules. Through the mouth of the wild boar he could see brother Marcel drawing the broadsword from Sir Ormerod's tomb. He gave it a comical flourish as the monks roared with laughter. He gave a friendly, half-apologetic smile as he bowed his great bulk with extravagant prissiness, and produced from his sleeve a silk glove which he cast onto the ground. Professor Quilloughby was upon him in a heartbeat, vaulting the ancient tomb of the knight, knocking the large man off his feet and pinning him to the ground. The broadsword clattered; the monks raised the roof with their cheering. Professor Quilloughby felt supportive hands on his back, heard congratulations muffled through his reeking headdress: 'well done, brother Percival!', 'now that's what I call playing by the book!' – but heeded none of them. Brother Marcel's panting, ruddy, bearded face beamed up at him through the beast's rotten fangs. He was on the cusp of saying something when the first tusk pierced his neck. His kind eyes bulged and he began to flail. The monks laughed and cheered again – the show gets better! But then brother Marcel began to gurgle. His limbs thrashed ever more weakly. Professor Quilloughby would not get up. Slowly it dawned on them. Cheers turned to screams of terror, hands once extended in filial respect attempted desperately to haul the savage creature from its prey. A dark stain spread over the straw. But the creature would not budge. Again and again it gored its victim with relentless tusks. And it did all this for the sake of politeness.

# THE COSMOLOGY OF PROSPER
# HARKNESS

There never was a more profitable place for a
dreamer to seek after strange tales than the Soho
auction parlour of Frantwhistle-Dent & Sons. Mr.
Rumbelow was not much of a dreamer, but even to
him the prospect of profit had a certain inalienable
charm. Strange tales, he thought, as he wafted
through the sale-room with practiced elegance,
might be sought elsewhere; might indeed be sought
successfully – but never quite so fashionably, quite so
deliciously as in the business of Frantwhistle-Dent &
Sons, esteemed purveyors of antique books.

It was a familiar hunting ground for Mr.
Rumbelow. Just as common foil sets off the sparkle

of a mounted jewel, so his close acquaintance with the scene, earned over many years of auction-mongering, made its curiosities stand out in starker and more brilliant relief. He had memorised the heraldries on its panelled walls. The arrangement of the viewing tables under whose glass the volumes, delicately spatchcocked, awaited the tenderisation of the auctioneer's gavel, was as familiar to him as a permanent collection to the curator of a museum. And much like this curator, every day walking the same halls and inspecting the same cabinets, Mr. Rumbelow found himself paying less and less attention to the actual artefacts on exhibit. He attended, increasingly, to those points of starkest relief. An observer, witnessing our portly gentleman weave through the aisles like a manorial spectre, might be inclined to take him for a dilettante – for such indeed he was. But Mr. Rumbelow's apparently apathetic review of the items on offer belied a scrupulous secondary analysis, a very careful registration of all the various booksellers, librarians and literati who filled the sale-room with whispers, their heads with subtle tactics, their auction catalogues with idiosyncratic glyphs in blunt pencil.

Mr. Rumbelow was mapping a topography of interest. He constructed a landscape of potentials, a landscape whose altitudes of curiosity were proportional to the volume of whispers in the sale-room, a landscape whose untrodden areas of research were inversely proportional to the crowd's own treading, re-treading, and clogging of the aisle. Mr. Rumbelow never entered the business of Frantwhistle-Dent & Sons with specific intentions. Such narrow methodologies, he firmly upheld, should be kept securely within the remit of the Faculty. All he needed was a few moments of mingling to know exactly where his own catalogue ought to be marked.

If Mr. Rumbelow was a dilettante, he was at least a curiously derived and baroque specimen of the genus. His tastes were eclectic, verging at times upon the heteroclite. He considered himself a latter-day antiquary and delighted in self-conscious archaism, which often drew him away from his University garret and towards such places where thereunto unsuspected cravings might be satisfied with the mysteries of mouldering MSS. A true intellectual gourmand, Mr. Rumbelow might fairly be said to possess a quite overpowering hunger for knowledge of any sort. But as a general rule, whatever seemed to be attracting the other buyers (and usually very clear islands of curiosity would resolve from the morass of pullulating patrons) was probably worth his attention.

This was not to say that Mr. Rumbelow was *entirely* directionless in his acquisitions. In fact, his attendance of this particular auction, the last one of the season, was an act of unusual premeditation. Should he return empty-handed, the winter would more than likely prove his intellectual starvation.

Mr. Rumbelow was a palaeographer by tenure, but a palaeontologist at heart. For him, the crust of the Earth was the richest of palimpsests. He had been an avid subscriber to the evolutionary record for many years, and where stratigraphic analysis was concerned, considered himself an accomplished 'lithorary critic'. And this particular auction, held on behalf of the Royal Society, consisting of the private library of a late Dr. Prosper Harkness (HonFRS), appeared uniquely adapted for his interests. He had even glanced through the catalogue beforehand.

The main attraction, he gathered very quickly, was a marvellously well preserved 2$^{nd}$ edition of Newton's *Principia* – and certainly the sale-room throng seemed concentrated around its little quarter of the viewing-table. It was a choice specimen, Mr. Rumbelow had to admit, probably rebound at some point in the late 18$^{th}$ century. And there were other islands of intrigue which tantalised him. A bespectacled fellow seemed unusually enthused by some annotations glimpsed in a minor geological treatise – which Mr. Rumbelow promptly noted as a point of interest. He had wondered in the past about the ethical dimension of his hunt, of his gluttony for noetic sweetmeats which sometimes verged on predation. If he swooped in to procure this treatise, might he be depriving that gentleman of some vital evidence? Might he be depriving the world of a revolutionary monograph for the sake of his own indulgence? But these had been a younger man's concerns. Now it was clear that the auction parlour of Frantwhistle-Dent & Sons was the forum for a sort of natural selection, a gauntlet of intense and continual competition: 'this law of battle', thought Mr. Rumbelow, in Darwin's own nomenclature. Nature herself, 'red in tooth and claw', had sanctioned his instinct to outbid all competitors. If he did not exploit his advantages, he reasoned, there was every chance that he would be expelled from his niche – deprived of his resources – and banished to the great library of fossils below. He circled the 'X' he had already made beside the catalogue entry for the geological treatise – and so began a very strange tale of his own.

To the errant palaeographer, the auction parlour and its exquisitely panelled sale-room were, as has been suggested, uncommonly familiar. But never in his wildest dreams did he expect so familiar a listing in the catalogue, a listing that (if indeed it was real) could only have succumbed to the eyeskip of his hasty foreinspection. Yet there it was. Right underneath that minor work by an imitator of Lyell. So familiar, and yet so enigmatic. It was the only book that Mr. Rumbelow had ever sought to win at auction – and failed. He brought a pudgy knuckle to his eye, and, finding it unencrusted with the sediment of dream, knew himself to be awake and lucid. Although Mr. Rumbelow had never so much as considered the possibility of such a thing, its reality could not be contested. The book had returned to him, as he had returned for it.

He checked the catalogue again and sounded the sale-room, surveying its contours of interest and noting a distinct and encouraging flatness around the table in question. Mr. Rumbelow's heart quickened as he navigated against the current of public interest, set single-mindedly on the close examination of this revenant fossil, this bizarre and mysterious volume which was listed only as *The Fanged Concepts*.

The catalogue described it thus:

*An unclassified MS from a collection of Dr. Harkness' personal affairs. In poor condition, heavy water damage and stains impinging from head and foot, heavy wear to artisanal binding. Possibly a private journal, undated and composed entirely in cipher with illustrations. 125mm x 200mm (approx.).*

An unusually meagre designation, but uniquely appropriate for the work concerned. It was the sort of cosmic *hapax* whose obscurity might occupy the mind of any mysteriarch for a lifetime – but specifically, thought Mr. Rumbelow, his own.

The first time the palaeographer had encountered *The Fanged Concepts* its association with Dr. Harkness had been quite meaningless, although the extraordinary strangeness of the artefact had enthralled him greatly. Truth be told, Prosper Harkness was still a rather puzzling figure, about whom the Royal Society spokesperson seemed almost contractually reticent – though now that the book's connection with the good doctor's scientific learning was all but confirmed, Mr. Rumbelow was doubly excited. It had appeared, perhaps half a year ago, in a collection of miscellaneous diaries sold for the benefit of that particular class of academic who, in delusions of scholarly mystique, would extract the empty bone-coloured pages of foolscap at the end and re-use them for their own ignoble purposes. Foolscap indeed, Mr. Rumbelow thought, for the coxcomb would not be far misplaced on the hollow heads of those who spent their time squabbling over empty pages in an antiquarian bookshop. In such impoverished company, he had thought that *The Fanged Concepts* (which did not contain a single unwritten page) would have made for easy pickings.

But he had been ambushed in his complacence – seized unawares by the apparently fathomless purse of an anonymous telegraph bidder – and he had gone hungry. For reasons Mr. Rumbelow could scarcely conjecture and dared not even question, it was clear now that whoever had enjoyed that early triumph had relinquished their prize. Now he could hunt without fear of mortal competition. He could at last strike his quarry without that dreadful and excruciating knot of antlers, the fight-or-flight engagements of the auction-house.

It was precisely where he thought it would be, illuminated softly beneath the glass of a long and promisingly unfrequented viewing-table. It was a scrappy little volume, he thought, the teal cover warped and wrinkled like the pelt of some rugose leviathan – but beneath this weathered integument, Mr. Rumbelow knew, there could be nothing other but the impeccably preserved soft tissues of a mystery. *The Fanged Concepts*. It was an unusual name – and, since the book itself was unmarked, a name whose origin would have to be uncovered. Perhaps the answer could be found amongst Dr. Harkness' papers, of which a medium-sized lockbox and several files were also on display, although something told Mr. Rumbelow that finding out would involve rather more than a simple cross-reference. To judge by the contents of his library as represented by the auction catalogue, Prosper Harkness was a man of very broad and unorthodox learning. Scientific treatises shouldered alchemical manuscripts and volumes of Symbolist verse, Vedic commentaries locked leaves with private noctuaries and, entertainingly, a late-mediaeval grimoire on the theme of 'necromancie'. Interest was everywhere divided, the landscape, riven with deep gorges of obscurantism and orogenic upthrusts of local curiosity – had never been more fractured at Frantwhistle-Dent & Sons. The answer had a hundred shades to hide in, but Mr. Rumbelow was not in the least dismayed. Instead, he was powerfully impressed by an abstract sense of fraternity, as if he and the dead doctor were somehow united in their pursuit – no, not quite pursuit, for 'pursuit' struck the meandering Mr. Rumbelow as an insufferably polar vector – rather, their *omnivorous accretion* of knowledge, which from opposite directions had somehow centred upon this same improbable tome. Mr. Rumbelow's mind began to salivate. It was quite clear that *The Fanged Concepts* were meant to be his.

The time of auction approached, and despite every favourable auspice, a vague feeling of anxiety had settled on Mr. Rumbelow. It was all the more noticeable for its unfamiliarity. The feeling had begun to nibble away at his innards ever since he had remarked, by dumb force of coincidence, the unexpected presence of *The Fanged Concepts* – and it had persisted, a chronic hunger-pang of the brain. He had reverted to that nervous habit of chewing his fingernails, or rather, his finger-nubs, which were already gnawed to the quick over a history of afternoons at Frantwhistle-Dent & Sons. At some point the prospective patrons arrayed themselves for auction, and, very much against his better judgement, Mr. Rumbelow steeled himself for competition. His instincts were lubricated by the sweat of apprehension, and as the auctioneer assumed his place, he felt himself bristling for dominance against an imaginary foe.

The alchemical scriptures, the Vedic annotations – all sold slowly and patchily; the *Principia*, as expected for a collector's piece, stirred the greatest storm of voices in the sale-room. Interest, as Mr. Rumbelow had correctly predicted, was exceedingly disparate. The sheer extent of Dr. Harkness' predilection for the obscure and arcane had evidently been equivocated by the spokesperson, but of course it was just this heterogeneity that Mr. Rumbelow cherished most. And now its exemplum had appeared on the podium. *The Fanged Concepts.* And at what a paltry appraisal! Mr. Rumbelow leapt to the slaughter. The book was like a prime cut, resting on the butcher's block – and destiny had conspired to make it his!

Another bidder raised their paddle. Not to worry, thought Mr. Rumbelow, a stray snipe, easily countered – until it came again. And again. And the asking-price rose with distressing alacrity.

Trying very hard to retain a placid demeanour, Mr. Rumbelow snuck a glance across the sale-room at his opponent – and powdered his teeth in despair. It was that wretch Mr. Philpott of Oxenford! In the cartography of curiosities, he was an eternal anomaly; forever muddying his co-ordinates with sophistic smokescreens, with ulterior motives and cloaked animosities. After months of being run up into alpine expenses, Mr. Rumbelow had come to know that, for Mr. Philpott, Frantwhistle-Dent & Sons was no perilous forum for natural selection – it was a drawing-room whist table. The two men furiously raised their paddles, a motion reflected increasingly by the auctioneer's eyebrows, and by the pencils of the crowd who were silently re-evaluating their thoughts on the runtish little curio. Higher and higher the numbers rose, and the red haze had fallen upon Mr. Rumbelow, the primal thrill of the hunt, the old adrenal rush – until at last the bludgeoning strike of the hammer fell, and fatally incapacitated his prey.

He could not resist firing a smug grin at his most unwelcome duellist – but Mr. Philpott was wearing one of his own. If that slimy devil had come in just to ruin him, thought Mr. Rumbelow – and quickly curtailed his thought. He was of a naturally competitive disposition, but not a wrathful one. And besides, under 'this law of battle', he had proved himself worthy. *The Fanged Concepts* were finally his. Mr. Rumbelow was so satisfied with the thought of his incumbent banquet, the luxuriant analysis of Dr. Harkness' bizarre manuscript, that he let the bespectacled geologist claim his marginal treatise unchallenged. In fact, Mr. Rumbelow was much too distracted to procure anything else from auction that fateful afternoon. And considering the great ransom he had forfeited, essentially on a whim, for an unknown work – perhaps that was for the better.

It was only after the sale, with his prize neatly packaged in brown paper and certified for authenticity, that Mr. Rumbelow suffered the pleasure of a direct encounter with Mr. Philpott. 'Morris Rumbelow!' the pale fellow exclaimed with the tremolo of an oaten pipe, 'good sport this afternoon, no?' The larger man inclined his stately bulk, exhibiting the full range of motion permitted by his rather outmoded three-piece. 'Good day, Quentin. Yes. Very good sport indeed'. A hackney-carriage should be approaching any minute, thought Mr. Rumbelow, as he made a sustained effort to identify one several streets away. Mr. Philpott was not perturbed. 'I couldn't help but notice' he continued, 'that you have made a very fine purchase today – yes, somehow that struck me as memorable. The item in question? Dr. Harkness' little folly – *The Fanged Concepts*. I'm afraid you'll think me awfully disreputable for saying so, Morris, but that strange little book is very important to me – the keystone to my research, I suspect'.

Mr. Philpott, a medical historian by office, was also an amateur oneirologist, whose promised masterwork on the history of dental imagery in dreams had buzzed in Mr. Rumbelow's ears every time they mischanced to cross paths at Frantwhistle-Dent & Sons. The very idea of it was tiresome. 'I was wondering', continued the irritant at his elbow, 'if I might have leave – with permission, of course – to consult it one of these days. I would account it a great kindness…' As he spoke these words, Mr. Rumbelow was inwardly celebrating the greatest victory his appetite had ever earned. His whole face warped into a caricature of generosity and, with syrupy, debonair malice, he handed his rival a visiting card. 'Perhaps, Quentin, perhaps…' he purred, 'when I have thoroughly finished reading it myself. I am quite a ponderous reader, I'm afraid – as you surely recall from our Eton days'. Mr. Philpott returned the sort of smile that very clearly broadcasted his opinion that Mr. Rumbelow's 'ponderous' deportment was no doubt a consequence of his ongoing enthusiasm for 'Eton' four square meals a day.

'I won't hesitate to call', he said, brandishing the card.

'Please do' said Mr. Rumbelow, as he hailed his hackney-carriage.

*** 

Mr. Rumbelow sat smoking a pipe in his University garret. It did not feel like much time had passed since the auction, though it had been several days. He had made precious little progress with his cryptic purchase, and still less with his official research, which, if one might be forgiven the fluvial metaphor, would have benefitted greatly from the brusque and numerous formation of ox-bow lakes.

But reminders of time's ever-rolling current were a ubiquitous feature in Mr. Rumbelow's quaint little chamber. On the wall hung a lithograph print of De la Beche's famous *Duria Antiquior,* and on the mantlepiece rested, like the great rib of a ship, the tibia of *Iguanodon* – itself, thought Rumbelow with rather too much pleasure, something of a Mantell-piece. A few of his own findings (including some wonderfully polished heteromorph ammonoids, a chunk of Rhynie Chert Prototaxites, and a quite singular imprint of a horsetail reed from the early

Mesozoic) were also displayed, between the jumbled strata of his many books, in small velvet-lined cabinets. All fine exhibits, he thought, from the ever-growing archive of the earth; the endless museum whose acquisitions were decided and curated, he knew, by the mighty stream of time. The palaeographer, whose amateur interests had led him to a serviceable understanding of the planet's geologic past, was very much aware of this. And yet it was still, in some sense, difficult to grasp. Working at a manuscript for several consecutive hours did very little to convince him that time existed beyond the present moment. He fantasised about it – a single, endless moment, where each peak and trough of one's eclectic interest might be mapped, without temporal inhibition, from all perspectives. If moments were perpetual, sequential – then one's experience of the world, thought Mr. Rumbelow, could only ever be as complete as the fossil record.

It was perhaps another uncanny coincidence that what little progress the palaeographer had made with *The Fanged Concepts* was deeply entangled with that same museum of petrified life he presently pondered. As per its listing, Dr. Harkness' book itself was encrypted in a maddening cipher – squiggles and spirals and fractalesque glyphs; a bizarre fusion of cave-wall ideographs with the line-forms of Futurist art, compounded at frequent intervals by numerous and utterly bizarre illustrations of what looked at times like animal teeth, at others like Polynesian war-clubs. The only comprehensible text Mr. Rumbelow had found was a sort of epigraph, carved into the leathern surface of the inside front cover:

*'Humanity must perforce prey on itself/*
*like monsters of the deep'.*

The rest of the manuscript was quite incorrigible – though this wasn't, of course, a deterrent to Mr. Rumbelow. If anything, the protraction of a mystery enriched its moment and made it all the more nourishing. Indeed, the difficulty of deciphering *The Fanged Concepts* had even proved strangely productive. Mr. Rumbelow had resorted to a more practical analysis of the artefact – in this case, a spot of chromatography, choosing for his sample a rather unobtrusive ink-stain on the eightieth page. Such processes were a staple activity for the seasoned palaeographer, who applied the requisite chemicals over a meal of eggs and toast – to quite a marvellous effect. A quick trip to the radiography lab had confirmed his conclusions. Dr. Harkness' mysterious journal was written in ink nearly two hundred million years old.

Extravagant indeed, given the volume required, but not revolutionary. Mr. Rumbelow knew it was possible to resuscitate the pigment from the fossilised ink-sacs of belemnites with a grindstone and a simple solution of ammonia. But it was still immensely curious. Subsequent tests revealed that the entire book was written in Jurassic tints. Was this simply an oddity of Dr. Harkness' method? His preference? Or did it serve some other function? Such delicious points of enquiry – not to mention, a great joy to find, that, much like himself, Prosper Harkness had dabbled in the depths of time. If the body of *The Fanged Concepts* treated a similar subject… Mr. Rumbelow would be very interested to find out. This book, with its prehistoric ink and primordial mysteries, might be as close as a textual holotype ever comes to a taxonomic one.

Mr. Rumbelow was just browsing through the final pages of his discovery when a knock came at his door. 'Come in', he said with a lazy puff of the pipe, and immediately regretted it when, in place of Elaine, his secretary, Mr. Philpott scampered into the dusky chamber.

'Quentin…' said Mr. Rumbelow, closing his eyes and his book, 'an unexpected pleasure'. Neither man moved. 'I happened to be in town', wheedled Mr. Philpott, 'and thought I'd drop by. I did inform the porters of my visit earlier this afternoon – but perhaps the news was waylaid… but never matter'. Mr. Rumbelow had in fact expressly informed the college that he would not tolerate any visits from a Mr. Quentin Philpott, who, he was sure, was perfectly cognisant of this circumstance. 'May I help you, Quentin?' asked Mr. Rumbelow, sinking further into his chaise lounge with a cumulus of pipesmoke. 'Have you made any progress with *The Fanged Concepts*, Morris? I'm awfully eager – with permission of course – to give it a read'. The portly gentleman gave a deep chuckle. 'Dear Mr. Philpott – I haven't even started. I am a very busy man – and while Dr. Harkness, whoever he was, must have been a very intelligent fellow – I daresay his prose leaves something to be desired.'

'Is that so…' said Mr. Philpott with an owlish look. Mr. Rumbelow had never enjoyed an encounter with his old rival quite as much as now… until Mr. Philpott spoke up. 'Very well, Morris. I suspect I shall have to look for answers elsewhere'. 'Elsewhere? Dear Mr. Philpott – I don't believe there's anything else in the world that might equal *The Fanged Concepts*'. 'Is that so?' asked the visitor again, as he produced a lockbox from his bag.

'What is that?' asked Mr. Rumbelow absently. 'Ah, nothing much – just some of Dr. Harkness' odds-and-ends which I managed to pick up from Frantwhistle-Dent & Sons. I'm surprised you didn't go for it yourself – this species of miscellaneous documentation seems right up your street'. Mr. Rumbelow emerged from the depths of the chaise lounge. He was – indeed – very surprised. 'Receipts and letter-drafts pulled off the good doctor's paper-spike, yes?' Now Mr. Philpott gave a chuckle. 'Not quite, Morris, not quite. A good deal of information, actually, and very important information at that'. 'What sort of information?' 'An address.' 'An address?' 'Yes. A contact to Dr. Harkness' estate and executor, who I will be visiting tomorrow, in fact, to uncover the mystery of *The Fanged Concepts*, as they say in the reading-room, *ad fontes*'. 'The mystery of *The Fanged Concepts*! Listen to yourself, Quentin. You've barely even seen the old book! What good can tracing it back to old Prosper's wet-nurse do when you don't have the faintest prospect-' 'Let me stop you there, Morris. You seem to know an awful lot about a book you haven't read – just like our Eton days, I suppose. And besides... I have these'. Mr. Philpott reached into the lockbox and withdrew, one by one, three large and obscenely formed fossils. Three *teeth*. Each one was stranger and more absurdly specialised than the last. Mr Rumbelow gave a start.

'These artefacts, conveniently included with the lockbox lot, are more than sufficient for my present research. No, Morris – you mustn't touch them. With these three splinters of bone, I have already come further than you in understanding the work of Dr. Prosper Harkness. And I don't mind telling you, as you will surely uncover yourself sooner or later – I made a brief detour to your radiography lab on my way up. These teeth are over six hundred million years old, Morris. Predating the Cambrian Explosion. And, if I'm to take the rather dumbfounded word of your experts at the Zoological Musery – they all belonged to *the same organism*'.

'Don't you have the facilities at Oxenford?' growled Mr. Rumbelow through pipesmoke. But he was utterly thunderstruck. The same organism? Six hundred million years old? Preposterous. The *jaw* itself was a Silurian innovation, four hundred and fifty million years young at the very least. And these teeth were so unbelievably complex, so specialised: honeycombed, ribbed and whelked with a cortical grain not wholly unlike those of *Labyrinthodont,* whose squat batrachian statue he had admired at the Great Exhibition. The simpering oneirologist was quite clearly bluffing, thought Mr. Rumbelow, this was an elaborate hoax and nothing further. But the more he looked at the teeth from the lockbox, the more he recognised them – the more he realised that Dr. Harkness' *illustrations* were in fact *diagrams*... and they had been drawn from the life. He exchanged his pipe for his fingernails.

'You're bluffing' Mr. Rumbelow sneered. Mr. Philpott gathered up the twisted tusks and closed the box. 'Now, Morris, I very much suggest you lend me your special little book. We can find a civil compromise, I'm certain – but it would save me a lot of time tomorrow. I entreat you – perhaps your co-operation will find you some credit in my breakthrough paper'. Mr. Rumbelow scowled through his pipe. 'Why don't you give me the address then, Quentin? A civil compromise, was it?' The other man laughed. 'Perhaps not quite *so* civil, Morris. It would be an awful shame for you, I suspect, to have your name smirched in my forthcoming publication – but I suppose I'll have no other choice. You are an impediment, Rumbelow, a stubborn obstacle – but not unnavigable. You can keep your *Fanged Concepts*. I'll still figure it out – before you'. Mr. Rumbelow narrowed his eyes. 'If you need it so much, Quentin – why, pray tell me, did you get rid of it before? Don't think I'm so dense, Quentin. You were that anonymous bidder, weren't you? I certainly don't recall exchanging our usual pleasantries that day. Why give it up, Quentin? Another trick for your ridiculous game?' The other man gave a comical look. 'Mr. Rumbelow, I have no idea what you're talking about. If somebody outbid you for the book half a year ago, I might advise that you finally get over it. And you never know – perhaps I shall find out about it tomorrow, at the Harkness estate. Tomorrow, Mr. Rumbelow. Good evening to you'.

And Mr. Philpott took his leave. Mr. Rumbelow was not a wrathful man. But he was a competitive one. *The Fanged Concepts* was, at its core, nothing but a pastime for him – a curiosity, a frivolous side-project to satisfy his terrible hunger for the esoteric and the obscure. But he had earned it, earned it through nature's irreducible axiom: the survival of the fittest. And this wretched scavenger, this opportunist, this mistempered link of the food chain, was threatening his place in the system. And that, for any lifeform, was not to be endured. But what could he possibly do? Tomorrow, Mr. Philpott would trace the work of Dr. Harkness to its source – its primal wellhead, unmentioned and seemingly unknown even to the spokesperson of the Royal Society – and there, no doubt, unravel it all. He seized *The Fanged Concepts* and rapidly scanned its final pages, desperate for the faintest morsel of advantage, the smallest orts and dregs of new understanding – and coming at last to the end of the book, found only a single blank page. He squinted. That was curious. He could have sworn the doctor's journal bore no such imperfection. Indeed, was that not precisely why it had been so unpopular with those wretched, patrician parchment-pinchers so many auctions ago? He squinted further – and gave a yelp of joy. Once more the jaws of coincidence had closed around him – once more the hinge of fate had found its fulcrum in the spine of Dr. Prosper Harkness' tome, whose tight-lipped covers, it appeared, might yet be prised apart in communication.

For there, pencilled in with spectral faintness, was an address – an address, no doubt, that had succumbed to the eyeskip of his much too hasty foreinspection. Mr Rumbelow had no other choice. Putting *The Fanged Concepts* in his satchel, he donned his greatcoat and summoned Elaine to summon his remise. Chance, he hoped, would continue to favour him, as he left that same night for the Harkness estate.

\*\*\*

The atmosphere bulged with bluish cloud as Mr. Rumbelow's carriage passed into the small coastal village of Bitmouth. Crepuscular rays fanned down from cracks in the heavy sky and made the rooftiles shimmer like the scales of some great recumbent reptile. The sea was the green hue of a sideways mirror, ruffled with foam like clustered florets of the saxifrage, the stone-breaker; blooming and dying with every breath of wind. Through the dormant streets the carriage rolled, and Mr. Rumbelow, only recently awoken from an unintended slumber, could see the stark cliffs rising sternly ahead, tufted with sand sedge and stunted heather bending in the salty wind. The beetling brows of each cliff-face were furrowed with geological strata – a severe and literal topography of interest, thought Mr. Rumbelow, but an unlikely place for the estate of a renowned scientist. He occupied the rest of the journey with studying *The Fanged Concepts*. The endeavour was, predictably, fruitless – though it continued to heap coals on the fire of his curiosity. His hunger for knowledge was keen; as keen, perhaps, as those bizarre teeth had once been, those teeth whose diagrams, worked in ancient ink, dangled before him as unreachable as the plutonic fruit of Tantalus.

He paid the coachman handsomely and disembarked. This tottering clifftop cottage, he had to assume, was the Harkness estate? A hollow formed in Mr. Rumbelow's stomach as he considered the likelihood that chance had forsaken him, that the address he had found was completely irrelevant, and that Mr. Philpott was – perhaps at this very moment – on his way to the right location, where the associates of Dr. Harkness would be able to help him with his ridiculous study. Mr. Rumbelow, in an uncommon oversight, had skipped his morning meal. He broke his fast on the fingernails of his left hand, as he knocked on the door with his right. There was no answer. He cursed his flesh-padded knuckles, and, bending down with extreme care for his joints and his suit – picked up a pebble, and knocked with it. He realised with some amusement that the pebble contained the whorl of a small ammonite – and then the door opened.

'Mr. Rumbelow?' came the voice from within. A very withered gentleman, shawled in a shapeless garment, was croaking up at him. Whether Mr. Rumbelow's weary mind failed to comprehend the strangeness of this greeting, or whether he simply refused to accept it, introductions were made with impeccable grace. The old creature gave a grin, and in the contest of erosion, his gums vied with the jagged cliffs below. 'Prosper Harkness' he said, extending a claw – 'do come in. I'll have to lock up behind us – else the wind will rattle so'.

The rickety cottage was built on two levels, the upper of which seemed quite securely barred. Mr. Rumbelow and his host sat sipping tea from chipped china, watching the waves roost and the sea-winds billow through a grimy bay window. 'I must say I was expecting you one of these days, Mr. Rumbelow. My agent was a very diligent cartographer of curiosity'. Mr. Rumbelow dumbly sucked at his brew and tried to pay attention to the shrunken anthroparion hunched across the table. This cottage was a true *lagerstätte* – a fossil-hunter's dream. Everywhere beautiful slabs of lias crawled with frozen life, oolites swarmed with tiny shells and shoeboxes brimmed with the black phosphatic teeth of prehistoric sharks.

The debris of chiselled belemnites was everywhere in evidence. He cleared his throat. 'Doctor – forgive my impudence – but I was very much under the impression… that you were deceased'. The old man smiled. 'Aye – for the best, that was'. 'But', Mr Rumbelow continued, 'it must have been *you* who outbid me for the book then, at the diary sale – at Frantwhistle-Dent & Sons?' Dr. Harkness' sunken eyes sparkled. 'The book?' asked Dr. Harkness, 'do you perhaps mean – *The Fanged Concepts*?'

Mr. Rumbelow opened his bag and placed the battered old tome on the table. The old man reached for it greedily, licking his shrivelled lips. 'I was hoping someone here could tell me about it', Rumbelow started, 'and – coincidence has favoured me profoundly thus far, I have to say, but never so much as this – there would be absolutely no-one better to ask than yourself'. Dr. Harkness seemed briefly to jitter with enthusiasm. 'I knew it would return to me', he whispered, and drew back his lips in another well-meaning rictus. 'Mr. Rumbelow, you have done me a great service… and it would be my honour to tell you the story of my little book'. 'Capital!' exclaimed Mr. Rumbelow, gulping with anticipation, as though for a lavish and much-delayed meal. 'But Dr. Harkness, forgive me, I must stress, before you begin – that I have felt, since I first laid eyes on the thing, a very curious connection – an affinity, one might say – as though you and I are much alike, and *The Fanged Concepts* – through what synchronicity I can only conjecture – has united us for a particular purpose… I too am a fossil-hunter, you see, of antiquarian disposition…' He trailed off as the old doctor twittered harshly. 'Perhaps that too will be explained, Mr. Rumbelow' he murmured, 'although I suspect you shall find it a tale of singular – dare I suggest superlative – strangeness'.

'*The Fanged Concepts* is a chronicle of my earliest breakthrough, the discovery of certain very unusual fossils off the Bitmouth cliffs. Fossilised teeth, they were – whose diagrams you will have seen in the book – unlike any others known to man. Every tooth different from the next. Structurally, almost impossible – morphologically, well now, who can say. There came a point where I realised that, with a handful of stone, I could rewrite the history of life on this planet. These fossils, you must understand, *should not exist* – much too complex… much too early. But the world of learning, I knew, was not ready for such upheaval – so I began devising *The Fanged Concepts* to keep my research secret until I had accrued enough evidence to support my discovery. And it was not long, Mr. Rumbelow, before the cliffs grew anxious under my interrogation, and gave up the evidence I needed, hah! – in the form of the coprolites.'

'Coprolites?' asked Mr. Rumbelow. Needless to say, he was rather in awe of Dr. Harkness – not only because the elusive scientist was, contrary to all expectation, alive – but because he so fully embodied the palaeographer's own values. He seemed to share that same voracious intellect, that rare mind which would readily exhume soup-bones from the *køkkenmøddinger* of bygone epochs to feed itself and grow fat with knowledge.

'Aye, coprolites – bezoars, excreta, call them what you will – the first real evidence for my great discovery – the true subject of *The Fanged Concepts*. A juvenile text, in the grand scheme of things – but the germs of it are all there'. 'The germs of what?' asked Mr. Rumbelow. 'My cosmology' replied Dr. Prosper Harkness, and as he did, a floorboard seemed to creak upstairs. 'To simplify matters, it transpired that these coprolites – coprolites, might I add, of highly anomalous composition – corresponded precisely to the date – aye, the apparently impossible date – of the teeth that I had previously discovered.' 'Six hundred million years ago...' 'Give or take. This was concrete proof – in candid carbon – that our conception of the deep time was woefully mistaken. That life – gigantic, complex life, to judge by the proportions of the teeth and, aye, what the coprolites show they had consumed – existed long before we thought it possible. Aeons, in fact, before anyone suspected it'. Mr. Rumbelow was intoxicated. The moment seemed to contract – and in that fossil-strewn cottage, the deep time was now.

'My conclusions, and their undeniable evidence, I presented to the Royal Society – expecting, foolishly, a rapturous reception. Of course, I received quite the opposite. I was named a charlatan, a sorcerer. My research was confiscated, and with it, *The Fanged Concepts*. How long this book rotted in some Royal Society vault I don't dare to speculate – but when I learned that the Society's fundraising auctions were stocked with its kind, I grew determined to buy it back – determined to complete my research. But my name was mud, Mr. Rumbelow. The Society had demoted me to an honorary fellowship, and even the government hiring office laughed in my face when I offered my services as a researcher – the *government hiring office*, Mr. Rumbelow!' The old man was becoming increasingly animated, his voice increasingly passionate. Little flecks of spittle were gathering in the coves of each jowl. 'I was forced to give up my estate and live like a recluse out here. Years I spent in this cottage – collecting fossils, pandering to passers-by and dilettantes – snakestones, verteberries, devil's fingers, pinecone-pebbles, aye, all for a pittance – to earn back *The Fanged Concepts* and convince the world of my cosmology. And it was during this time

– aye, perhaps two years into my exile – that I made the greatest discovery of my life – perhaps of my field, nay, the greatest discovery in scientific history!'

Mr. Rumbelow was slightly taken aback by the old man's mounting fervour. He hesitated before asking the obvious question, although his host barely seemed to hear.

'A tempest broke her landfall over Bitmouth, aye. The heavens gaped wide. Great rains smote the cliffs from above, waves gnawed from below – and the great stone sundered, split off into the boiling torrent. Next morning, I went out to survey the havoc – and there it was, bare and exposed in the cliff-rock, picked clean by the ravening elements. My greatest discovery. A *complete skeleton*'.

'Do settle down a moment, Dr. Harkness – you've spilt your tea. A complete skeleton? I'm not certain I follow...' The shrivelled old man leapt up from his armchair and barked with hoarse laughter. Outside, the wind licked, the ocean seethed in silent, pulsing peristalsis.

'Aye, you heard me, Rumbelow! A complete skeleton – the keystone of my infant cosmology – and, earth and sky protect me, all those *teeth*... thousands of them! Millions! In every imaginable size and form – and, gods above and below, *all those jaws*... aye, I had found it! *Proteodontus* – for its fangs of sundry shape, of course, but also after

Proteus, you see, for its gift of knowledge… all its delicious, flawless, ancient, knowledge!' Mr. Rumbelow was becoming rather alarmed. 'Now see here, Dr. Harkness – is this not rather excessive? I am all for strange tales – in fact, I account myself a connoisseur – but Doctor, contain yourself! A story can only go so far!'

'The mouth, Mr. Rumbelow, the maw – is the site of consumption, yes, but also of communication. I have seen the bones of a god, Mr. Rumbelow – and they spoke to me! Yes, they revealed everything! The fossils chattered, Mr. Rumbelow – they taught me things that *The Fanged Concepts*, a mute and teething babe, had barely begun to understand…' The old man clutched his book and gave a wicked grin, 'but necessary for my studies' he crooned. 'I had my agent scour every catalogue he could find until it reappeared at auction. By then I had earned enough to procure it – in spite of your efforts, might I add, to bankrupt me in the process! I was able to return to my estate, and get back to work deciphering the mysteries of *Proteodontus* – until the great mandibles of the trap clamped shut. My reacquisition of *The Fanged Concepts* had not gone unnoticed by some old enemies at the Royal Society. I was forced to abandon it all – my research, my library, my estate and all earthly contact – in short, to falsify my own death – if I was to make sure my true discovery remained safe – remained secret. Hah!' spat Dr. Harkness, 'and it worked! I have been holding court with *Proteodontus* ever since – and very soon, now that my book has returned, I shall be ready to publish our extended dialogues. The whole world shall recognise the cosmology of Prosper Harkness!'

Mr. Rumbelow stood up abruptly. 'I think I've heard enough, Doctor. While exotic, I fear this knowledge is somehow spoilt – certainly my appetite has suffered tremendously.' 'What do you know of appetite, Rumbelow?' the maniac snapped, 'What do you *know* of anything? Sit down. You will learn today. Do you know what Wald wrote about the eye, Mr. Rumbelow? "A very narrow window through which at a distance one can see only a crack of light. As one comes closer the view grows wider and wider, until finally through this same narrow window one is looking at the universe". I will show you the universe, Mr. Rumbelow, and the universe is *devouring itself*. Darwinian evolution, hah! An insufferable polar vector! The Many Jawed One has showed me everything – has shown me time, the eternal moment, stretching infinitely in *both directions*, past and future, aye, *contracting*, slowly snapping shut like a pair of jaws, forever chewing away at the gristle of our biology, forever narrowing the pathetic pinhole of our mortal comprehension! Every second is a lost history, and every fraction of every second is an inwards-facing fang of the universe, plunging deeper and deeper into our substance, whittling us down into death – into fossils – into the ultimate petrifaction, cosmic entropy! I have found the bones of the ouroboros which is the universe, Mr. Rumbelow, and I have spoken to each of its many mouths. *Proteodontus*! O Many Jawed One! High Priest of VUUNTH!'

The doctor was howling and gnashing the air in profane ecstasy when Mr. Rumbelow decided enough was enough. The man was clearly insane – and he could keep his miserable book! With a brisk farewell he had moved to the cottage door – and found it locked. Another heavy creak came from the floor above, and Dr. Harkness, clutching *The Fanged Concepts*, was blocking the corridor. 'You don't believe me, Morris? You don't see the enclosing maw of reality? The coincidences that occur when molars interlock? When canids clasp at the flesh of all things, the carnivorous pincer of time? I tell you again, Morris Rumbelow – *I knew you would bring me this book!*' 'How!?' wailed Mr. Rumbelow, 'How!? Let me out of this awful place! You are mad! You are *mad!*' Dr. Harkness flashed a wretched grin – his teeth were long and dreadful. 'The Many Jawed One told me *everything*, Mr. Rumbelow. But I suspect you still don't believe me. Come upstairs. This shall be a practical education – with choice readings, aye, from

*The Fanged Concepts*! Is that not what you came here for? All-consuming knowledge? Hah! Upstairs, Mr. Rumbelow! The Many Jawed One shares your hunger!'

\*\*\*

It was lunchtime when Mr. Philpott arrived at the quaint little clifftop cottage, lockbox, papers and fossils in tow. Poor old Mr. Rumbelow, he thought; always taking competition much too seriously. The upcoming publication would rip him to shreds! Perhaps that would caution him, thought Mr. Philpott, for always thinking with his mind's stomach. The oneirologist knocked. He had never met his employer before, though he had served him for some years – and was ready to claim payment for the delivery of *The Fanged Concepts*, which, if he was any true judge of his old rival's character, would certainly have happened by now. He had taken a risk not giving him the address, but Dr. Harkness – whose prescience was, at times, disturbingly reliable – had assured him it was unnecessary. The only payment Mr. Philpott sought, of course, was a spot of help with his floundering paper. The mysterious old scientist, he knew, was both an expert dreamer, and an expert on... highly unusual dentistry. But what *was* that horrible racket? He knocked again on the door, and the whole structure seemed to knock back at him.

Mr. Philpott walked around the cottage. He reached a rather grimy seaward window, and peeked inside – recoiling instantly, retching, gagging in horror and disgust. He had locked eyes with a hideous old man, and – without stopping even to think, Mr. Philpott had fled down the cliffside road and into Bitmouth, howling all the while for the doctor, the constable; imploring wildly unto the wind for 'anyone!' until at last attention came. When Bitmouth's lone police officer and two young fishermen arrived with an iron crow to breach the cottage door, the clamour had stopped – and an eerie stasis filled that house of remnants. Nothing remained to witness but a silent, sculpted echo of life – an imperfect record of that mortal chaos which Mr. Philpott swore he had glimpsed only moments ago.

Downstairs, an old hermit had plainly murdered himself – although his methodology quite perplexed pathologists the county over. His stomach, a raw and bloated haggis, was stuffed with a hideous melange of inky woodpulp, teal leather and ragged flesh. The autopsy report registered a quite unprecedented cause of death: 'suicide by autophagy'.

The scene upstairs was still more baffling. All that occupied the attic room was a heaving ossuary of gnawed and carious bones, apparently in a state between death and petrifaction. It was speculated that the reclusive old fossil-hunter was assembling a dinosaur, but none of the men could exactly imagine *what* the jumbled beast was supposed to have looked like. Lively debate as to the nature of the 'Bitmouth remains' is known to entertain the Royal Society to this very day. And of the hundred thousand alien fangs which shared that chamber, Mr. Philpott would not speak a word. He cast the lockbox and all its contents into the sea, trying very hard to forget that half-handful of uncommonly white – uncommonly small – and uncommonly *human* teeth that glinted among the rest, like recent acquisitions in a great and terrible museum.

# THE FÊTE OF ZAGREUS

Lionel Raddlescott sat sternly in his spartan lodgings, contemplating the tyranny of material objects. The run-down little cottage was quiet and empty of all but the meanest accoutrements – but the cottage was not the subject of his meditations. Through the sunken glaucoma-coloured window he could see the tyrants, robed in great palliaments of tarpaulin, standing stark and imperious among the weeds of the barren field. He could not remember a time in which they had not dominated his thoughts, a time in which they had not inspired in his soul a deep and thoroughly unmatched abhorrence. For it was under the yoke of these tyrants that his family had been enslaved for generations. With each generation the suffering had increased and the reward had diminished. And now, with his father's death, Mr. Raddlescott had sensed the first real chance he'd ever had to cast off their cruel, enduring subjugation – and give his own son the gift he'd been denied. A free existence. He stared at his oppressors, shapes distant and menacing in the blasted field, and grimly pondered the ways in which he might escape them.

He knew that it was not uncommon for people to feel haunted by the obligations of a family business – particularly if it happened to be an illustrious or longstanding one. Many children had been, like him, coerced by anxious fathers and grandfathers into wasting their youth 'learning the ropes' of some passionless toil, all in the interests of assuring them that their own misspent lives had not, in the end, been entirely in vain. Sadly enough this was a common occurrence. What was less common, thought Mr. Raddlescott, was to have a family business inextricably shackled to several tonnes of outmoded and now almost entirely dysfunctional machinery. It was easy enough for young pariahs to defy tradition and walk away from a more conventional family firm: a village shop, say, or (heaven forbid) a legal office. But it had been simply impossible to walk away from the Raddlescott Family Faire. The monkey on his back was dressed in several miles of tattered motley and weighed as much as a small battleship. In his great-grandfather's time, people had called it a risky investment – though the early successes of the enterprise proved a great vindication. But with every passing year, the rides grew less exciting and more expensive to repair. The Ferris wheel, which had once been the Faire's most popular attraction, had been sold early on to maintain solvency after a particularly bad season – but by the time Mr. Raddlescott's father inherited the business, it was tottering on its last legs. Growing up he had watched its desolation encroach from behind unvisited amusement booths and candyfloss machines that spun only cobwebs. He had been told time and time again that it was his duty to carry the torch; that only he could resurrect the great family business; that he had no choice in the matter. How he hated it. And now he had inherited its great metal bones.

They tyrannised him from beyond the grave. Monumental reminders of the shattered legacy to which he was chained. There was the rat-eaten big top that even as a boy he had never seen unfurled. There was a carousel missing half its team of horses – in a fit of desperation, his father had sold them to a collector of fairground memorabilia, and so hamstrung any attractiveness the attraction might once have possessed. There were the struts and awnings of the many stalls from which village craftsmen and farmers and even small-time entrepreneurs had once paid a small commission to hawk their produce. With dwindling crowds, the commission had seemed steeper every year, until eventually it was much too steep. There were the skeletons of a few children's rides, whose once-bright innocence seemed particularly mournful now that they were overcast with rust and ruination. And there was the Ziggurat. It was the arch-despot of that all oppressed Mr. Raddlescott, the dark tower whose hail of debris every day placed another stone on the wicked cairn of material objects that pinned down his struggling soul. Almost forty feet in height, the Ziggurat in its prime had dispensed more excitement than any other amusement in the Raddlescott Family Faire. After climbing its steep and rickety zigzag of tread-plate stairs, thrillseekers would be strapped into the open cockpit and – after an excruciating and unpredictable delay – would be sent plummeting to the ground, only for disaster to be averted at the last second by an ingenious system of steel cables and pulleys. In its current condition, of course, the Ziggurat was a death-trap, held together not by rivets and weldments, but by ivy and creepers. And it perfectly exemplified Mr. Raddlescott's torturous conundrum. He was paralysed. He couldn't sell the Ziggurat – not only on account of its lethality, but because of its archaism. Newer versions of the ride had dispensed with the unsightly stairway and could be boarded at the base from a cockpit subsequently winched skywards. There could be no demand for such a thing, even among fairground owners. He couldn't even sell it for scrap – rusting in a field on the outskirts of the village, nobody would transport the massive thing. Repairs were out of the question. Not only would they cost a fortune, but the majority of the Ziggurat's components had been discontinued from factory production. And even if it were to be fixed, the only way that Mr. Raddlescott could turn a profit was by renting it to other fairgrounds or (even worse) reviving the Raddlescott Family Faire – and so prolonging his bondage to all that he wished to escape. It was a thoroughly miserable state of affairs. But the otherwise unfortunate fact of his inheritance had a silver lining. If any opportunities arose to rid himself of the terrible burden, he at last had the power to take them. It remained his eternal duty to seek out, or if possible, *contrive* such opportunities. Which is precisely what came to pass that afternoon, when Lucian came home from the village.

Lucian Raddlescott was an elfin child of twelve or thirteen. His eyes were wide with a rare wonder at the world and all that it contained – which was a perpetual source of unease for his father, whose own severe and cynical squint was designed to strain everything out of the universe except its most threatening shadows. Even on dry days Lucian's boots tracked mud, and his pockets bulged with curiosities mineral and natural he had found on his trips to and from the village library – curiosities whose wonders he had long ago learned not to share with his father, for fear of another lecture about the 'tyranny of material things'. Lucian, of course, could not wrap his head around this. The only tyrant in his life was the man who spent all day staring out the window scheming over the things that he hated, the man who never missed an opportunity to take that hatred out on him. Just that afternoon Lucian had crept quietly through the door and was peacefully making his way through the barely-furnished sitting room when his father's voice came from the chair. 'What's that you've got there Lucian? Show me'. The boy guiltily unbuckled his satchel and presented the spoils of the day. It was a brown-covered library book: *Mysteries of Antiquity*. Mr. Raddlescott scrutinised it severely. 'And what else?' he asked with stony dispassion. The boy's expression of guilt intensified – or perhaps it was tinctured with shame at the failure of his ruse. He produced another book, finer and slenderer than the first, from the inner pocket of his satchel. *The Orphic Hymns*. His pale hand quivered like a flower. 'This isn't a library book' said his father, 'where is the label? Where is the stamp?' 'The librarian said I could have it' whispered

Lucian, 'she gave it me as a gift, on account of how much I liked reading it'. Mr. Raddlescott seemed to fill the room. 'Lucian, Lucian…' he quietly sorrowed, cradling his head in his hands, 'you are my son and for that I will always love you. But you are a fool, and for that I have a mind to tan your foolish hide. How many times have I warned you about the *tyranny of material things*? Of material things, Lucian, books are among the worst. They multiply so quickly. Maybe you read one book, maybe two, suddenly you have a fancy to read more books and before you know it we have a library on our hands. And then what? Then we're hemmed in by books from wall to wall, we can't do anything but breathe stale book-air, our minds are filled with books, and when you die someone will be lumped with all your books and they won't be able to do anything with them and they'll suffer for it and it'll be your fault. I've said it once and I'll say it again. This is the rule: only one book at a time in this house, and only books from the library. Do you hear me?' 'But dad', said Lucian, '*you* have two books – there's the bible in the bedstand, and the book with all the notes and numbers that you keep in-' 'That's enough, Lucian. I want you to take this book back to the library. Tell the librarian that your father already bought you a copy. Is that understood? I cannot bear to see my own son fall foul of this terrible trap', he spat, suddenly wroth, 'this addiction to baubles and trinkets that brings only servitude. Is that understood?' Lucian assented, but he did not understand. If anything, books struck him as a good solution to the so-called 'tyranny' that his father kept harping on about. Lost in the pages of a good book, the material world and all its tyrannous 'things' exerted no influence over him whatsoever – his mind was free to rove as it pleased in strange and ancient places, which were his favourite things to read about. Quietly he suspected that his father would do well to read a book or two himself, although of course he wouldn't dare mention such a thing. In fact, Lucian thought, now was the perfect time to change the subject – before his father's rage had reached its natural climax, and before he had inevitably catalysed its passage there with further 'foolishness'. 'If I go back to the library now', he asked timidly, 'can I stay out this evening to watch the Turanians?'

'The Turanians?' asked Mr. Raddlescott with surprise. He had been caught quite off guard. Lucian inwardly smiled at the success of this little manoeuvre. 'Yes', he said with sparkling eyes, 'I saw the line of caravans coming in, like a fallen rainbow snaking along the ground'. For as long as anyone could remember, the Turanians had come through the village every few years with their travelling circus. The villagers called them Turanians because it sounded knowledgeable and specific, even though it wasn't. The fact of the matter was that nobody had the first clue where the travellers came from, except that it was far away. But that was beside the point. They called their circus the Fête of Zagreus, and it was unlike any other circus in the world. It was legendary. The Fête of Zagreus was so popular that the Turanians never left a village they visited without taking a few people with them: dreamers, mostly, young lads and lasses lorn with wanderlust, seduced by the richness and novelty of their nomadic life. As for why exactly the Fête enjoyed such popularity, Mr. Raddlescott was mystified. It was apparently frowned upon to discuss what actually *happened* in each performance – and the performances themselves, to the man's increasing mystification, were completely free, with the only condition being that all who attended were expected to participate. It was an avant-garde, foreign notion of entertainment with which Mr. Raddlescott was not entirely comfortable. As a child, of course, he had never been allowed to join in the Fête of Zagreus – after all, the Turanians were competitors, and it would be ill to 'defect', as his father had once said with all the savagely misplaced allegiance in his heart, 'to cosy up with outsiders and put your own blood out of business. For shame'. Some lingering loyalty had so far forbidden him to let Lucian attend the festivities – although once, long ago, they had spent the night out upon the hill together, counting Turanian cookfires. That was before he had realised the extent of these outsiders' obsession with gewgaws. His father had always waxed hyperbolic in descriptions of their strange habits, an affectation of which the austere Mr. Raddlescott now strongly disproved – describing how their convoy swept up trifles like a great magnet: old cauldrons and gallipots for the mending, the spindled skeletons of old umbrellas with which they were always tinkering and trading.

And so retracing the path of elder bigotries, the manacles of Mr. Raddlescott's mind began to jangle. In fact, he could almost feel them coming loose. An idea was beginning to form. If but a fraction of his father's exaggerations were true – if the Turanians really were, even partly, a band of mendicant junk traders – upon who better, he schemed, could he foist the wreckage that so oppressed him? They would be easy to swindle, he reasoned, coming from afar, and with such a fervent appetite for the yoke of material things! He turned to Lucian, his gaze flashing icy with calculations. 'Yes, lad. You can go and see the Turanian camp this evening. And I shall go with you'.

\*\*\*

If Lucian's eyes were known to grow wide over interestingly shaped pinecones and unusually coloured stones, very little could have prepared him for the wonder of the Turanian camp that evening. They approached it together, seeing the great curving line of curiously wrought caravans and laden wagons drawn close together as if curling up to sleep. Fires were blazing in great bronze braziers, and Lucian could with excitement discern the dark groups of strange men and women ringed around them, sitting cross-legged on rich blankets and divans. Nearby an untied pony was rolling itself languidly in the long grass, and as he walked closer Lucian marvelled at the sight of two shaggy-maned horses with a more than trivial strain of zebra in their blood. They passed a covered wagon where a woman was arranging ceramic pots of liquor. She smiled at him, flashing a gold tooth, and Lucian turned his eyes with a blush. A caracal hissed from a bamboo cage. The camp was utterly mesmerising, he thought – as though it had come directly from the pages of a book. 'Tekeli', they heard a man call, 'we have guests'.

Lionel kept his hand firmly on his son's shoulder, though he felt the boy trying to shrug. He squinted at the Turanian campsite with suspicion – mixed, Lucian thought, with a little glint of excited calculation, when his eyes lit upon a wagon pendant with metal items brassy and shimmering in the firelight. A sallow youth guided them, weaving between brazier and bedroll and a great many wonders half-glimpsed in the golden gloam, until they reached a man who sat smoking a cheroot in the beautiful, tasselled mouth of a caravan. The air was sluggish with an incense that made Lucian's nose tingle. The man stood up and welcomed them, gesturing to a pair of ottomans at his feet – 'please, sit down, and make yourselves at ease' he said in a voice like silk. Mr. Raddlescott immediately took this Tekeli fellow to be some sort of ringleader for the Fête of Zagreus – and raised his social defences in preparation. Lucian, however, had been utterly enchanted. When the man had stood up to move closer to his sitting guests, the boy had glimpsed into the caravan behind him – and seen the books, so many books, more rare and more beautiful than the ones in the library; all in spiced leather, their fat spines fretted with arabesques of gold. He barely suppressed a gasp – although it made so much sense, given what he had seen of the camp, that the Turanians loved to read. He was in awe also of the man whose books they were. His beard was long and black and glossy: his wavy hair was still longer and glossier with tiny beads in it that glimmered like the stars, subtly rose and green and gold beneath their shine. He gave Lucian a winning smile. And then the two men began to talk.

'The carousel', his father was saying, 'just needs a lick of paint – works as well as the day it was made…' The Turanian man was nodding sagely, a glow of intent behind his sharp, dark gaze like the reflector of a gas lamp. Lost in his reverie, Lucian was startled to notice that a hairy creature in a ratty velvet waistcoat had come to hunker beside him. It was an ape – perhaps a chimpanzee, about his own size. Lucian had never seen such a beast before. He had read once that chimpanzees belonged to the genus 'Pan', and indeed there was a faunish mischief about this fellow that did not fill Lucian with an enduring sense of comfort. He shifted slowly towards his father and the ape shifted with him, mimicking the way he sat with uncanny accuracy. 'Don't mind Mister Wrinkles', smiled the Turanian, 'he doesn't have any teeth'. The ape gave a low and wistful hoot, as if he too was sharing in Lucian's revelry. 'The Ziggurat', his father was saying, 'is in almost perfect order. Sure it's got a bit of wear and tear, but nothing that your folk can't fix in a jiffy'. From the depths of his robe, the man they called Tekeli pulled out a green bottle, which Mr. Raddlescott brusquely refused. He offered it to Lucian, who could feel his father tensing. Lucian accepted with a quiet 'thank you' and took a sip. The bottle was elaborately carved, seemingly from a single green crystal, at which he would have liked to marvel longer. The liquor inside was syrupy and spiced and made his senses sing. Mr. Raddlescott cleared his throat sternly. Lucian made to give the bottle back, but the Turanian gestured with his eyebrows to Mister Wrinkles, and Lucian cautiously passed it over to the chimpanzee, who happily wrapped his lips around the neck. The scene was so fantastical that Lucian began softly to laugh. He could feel his father bristling with hostility, but because the general atmosphere of the Turanian camp had already guaranteed another tirade on the theme of material tyranny, he didn't see why he shouldn't abandon himself a bit while he still had the chance. 'How much do you want for all this?' asked the man with the silken voice. 'For you', said Mr. Raddlescott impressively but unconvincingly, 'five hundred pounds'. Secretly of course he was prepared to accept any price. The Turanian composed himself with a sort of feline majesty. In the firelight, thought Lucian, he looked a bit like one of the Three Wise Men from the nativity story he had learned about in school, when he wished they had played a larger role – being by far the most interesting characters. 'I will gladly accept your offer', he said slowly, 'if you will give us your boy, and let him join the Fête of Zagreus. If he is eager, of course'.

Mr Raddlescott nearly leapt up from his ottoman. 'Preposterous!' he nearly shouted, nearly following up with a stream of choice invectives about the Turanians and their thraldom to tat and rubbish. Lucian nearly also leapt up – 'I *am* eager!' he nearly shouted with joy. It was as though he had opened a book to find not a page but a doorway to another world – and if such a thing had happened, as he so often wished it would, he wouldn't think twice about leaving his life behind. But his father's hesitation had affected him in some strange invisible way. He seemed to be really *thinking* about it – which was disturbing to consider, no matter how badly he wanted to go. In spite of everything, he had thought his father loved him. *I love him*, thought Mr. Raddlescott, *I only want what's best. Am I not making this bargain for his sake? So that the boy doesn't inherit my burden, so that he can live a free and happy life? But isn't that what the Turanian is offering him – offering us both? Without Lucian I will be free from the tyranny of material things – and he will be free to collect his trinkets without strife...*

'I don't think-' began Mr. Raddlescott, as Lucian quietly interjected. 'It's alright, dad. I'll go'.

Lionel Raddlescott was at once relieved that the choice had been made for him, elated to be free at last of his ancestral subjugation, betrayed that his son had forsaken him for the inverse of all he stood for, inherently suspicious at the deal, and angry because that was his permanent condition. 'Lucian', he said sternly, 'you will do as I say. Will he be free to leave your little troop as he pleases?' Tekeli laughed. 'Many people run away to the circus. You'd be amazed at how many people run away from it. We're not an average circus troop, Mr. Raddlescott. There are no wages and no treacherous contracts in the Fête of Zagreus. Your boy – Lucian – will be free at all times to do precisely as he desires'. Mr. Raddlescott pretended very hard to consider. Lucian was aware of this, and even Mister Wrinkles gave his belly a theatrical slap.

'You may go', he said at last, 'indulge your adolescent fancies for a season, but you must return home next year. Is that understood?' Used to his father's arbitrary impositions, Lucian assented. He was awestruck in the face of the agreement, if a little crestfallen that it had not been harder for his father to choose between his pathological asceticism and his own son. Yet he could not help but feel that the outcome had been favourable for them both. 'Then let it be settled' said the Turanian, shaking Mr. Raddlescott's hand. 'I will send men to gather the machinery right away; they will toil through the night. Lucian will stay with me. I will show him the convoy and the camp. And tomorrow you will attend the Fête of Zagreus on its opening night of the season. No, I insist – you shall be the guest of honour. May it ratify our exchange', he said, robbing Mr. Raddlescott of his choice in the matter, and standing up to bid him farewell. The sallow youth, who had been waiting in the shadows, disappeared into the caravan and returned with a small chest – the agreed payment. 'Be good, Lucian' said Mr. Raddlescott flatly. 'I will', said Lucian, embracing his father. 'Well met', said the Turanian with effortless grandeur, gently taking the boy's hand. And as Mr. Raddlescott left the chaos and clutter of the camp with the chest under his arm, he could hear the eager hooting of the chimpanzee; beneath it the Turanian's warm, rich laughter, and beneath it the chimes of his son's own changeling throat.

\*\*\*

That night Mr. Raddlescott sat facing the window, and did not sleep. He could hear the Turanians jabbering away in their strange foreign tongue. He could hear the trot and whinny of horses dragging away their spoils – and now and then, punctuating the night, he could hear the crash and clatter of wicked idols tumbling to the ground. It was the blissful sound of tyrannicide. He wished he could watch it happening, see them take the Ziggurat to pieces and bear it back to the camp – but had it not been his desire all along to be content with absence? The Turanians had done him a great favour by paying in pieces of unminted gold. He would never be tempted to spend it, and so commit again the folly of whichever bygone relative had decided to invest their fortunes in the condemnation of their descendants to eternal servitude. Five hundred pounds in gold, and freedom. Had it been worth the sound of his son's stealthy footfalls in the doorway? His quiet and obedient 'goodnight, dad?' But Lucian too, Mr. Raddlescott reminded himself, had achieved freedom of a kind. What more could he have asked? Even if the Turanians reanimated the bones of the Raddlescott Family Faire, it could not exert its influence over him. It belonged, now, to the Fête of Zagreus. The Fête of Zagreus, he recalled, which he had promised to attend tomorrow evening, for the first time in his life. Certainly, he was apprehensive – he would have preferred to avoid all further contact with the Turanians, his swindle notwithstanding. Eventually Mr. Raddlescott drifted off to sleep, and liberated at last from the chains of his childhood, he did not dream.

The time had come to visit the Fête of Zagreus. Mr. Raddlescott had dozed until the afternoon, waking with a strange feeling in his bones. Not exactly regret – but a sort of emptiness. Without the tyranny of material objects upon which to focus all his thoughts and feelings, he felt strangely incomplete. With a pang he realised that he was already beginning to miss Lucian. The cottage, dull and devoid of all decoration, had never seemed emptier. Their farewell, perhaps, had been altogether too brief. Putting on his plain, respectable jacket, Mr Raddlescott resolved to seek out his son at the Fête that evening, and make the necessary amends.

Coming over the hill, he was mildly horrified to see that the enormous mouldering big top that had once belonged to the family business was erect and streaming particoloured pennants. It had been patched up with motley squares, and around it the Turanian wagons had been arranged in a great circle, braziers still blazing like beacons around the rampart of a ludicrous mock-fortress. He had realised, the night before, that they were not in fact cookfires. To whichever strange creed the Turanians belonged, they did not eat meat. Even in the fading light of dusk, he could distinctly see the villagers milling around the entrance. He joined them, furtively stealing glances into every caravan he passed for a glimpse of Lucian. 'Didn't expect to see you here, Lionel!' said the baker, 'it's so good that you've come – they've really upscaled this year, what with the new tent and all'. Mr. Raddlescott afforded him the sort of smile in which only the chronically charitable would misinterpret any measure of friendliness. His distaste for Turanian opulence was well known in the village. But before he could suffer any other recognitions, the pavilion draperies were drawn open and the visitors began to file slowly inside. Lucian was nowhere to be seen. Perhaps he was already within, having been recruited to help with the night's performance. The closer Mr. Raddlescott came to the entrance, the more clearly he could hear a strange sort of music – a charivari of concertinas, fiddles, pots and pans. Was that a lyre, buried amongst it all? He rolled his eyes. A reverential hush seemed to fall on every villager as they passed into the pavilion. And finally his turn had come.

He found himself in an atrium, partitioned from the main chamber by walls of canvas. A brazier choked the air with fragrant incense. A Turanian man sat behind it, a great bag by his side and a ceramic vessel between his feet. Mr Raddlescott realised with dread that the man was wearing a painted mask, a mask representing a goat with twisting horns. Was the acclaimed Fête of Zagreus really just some infantile masquerade? He groaned inwardly. 'Take off your boots' the masked figure said. Mr Raddlescott was about to protest this ridiculous rubric when he remembered his promise, and the line of villagers waiting impatiently behind. He put his boots neatly by a great pile of footwear massing in the corner. The masked figure reached into the vessel and drew forth a frothing cup, beautifully carved as if from a single green stone. The ostentatious objecthood of the thing made him shudder. 'All who cross the threshold must partake of the holy Kykeon', the figure intoned. 'I really don't think that's-' '*all* who cross the threshold', he repeated, 'into the domain of Zagreus'. This is the sort of childish make-believe that Lucian would fall for in a heartbeat, realised Mr. Raddlescott – when his head wasn't deep in a book, it was high in the clouds. He took the cup and downed the syrupy mixture with disgust. The figure reached into his bag and pulled out a painted mask. A scowling bull. He gave it to Mr. Raddlescott who, now thoroughly resigned to his immediate fate, put it on with scarcely a quibble. How could people actually *enjoy* this farce? The mask was awkward and stifling, a coloured cloth covered the back of his head and restricted the flow of air. Already the warmth was uncomfortable. The goat-man was speaking to him in a memorised, mystical cant. 'Supplicant', he said, 'walk free and be welcome to the Fête of Zagreus'. And he let Mr. Raddlescott pass through into the main chamber.

Here the music and the heat and the incense was at its most oppressive, and Mr. Raddlescott was taken aback by the bewildering whirl of an immense ring-dance whose steps everyone instinctively appeared to know but him. Sweating beneath his respectable jacket, he peered from his uneven eyeholes to see a troop of dancing girls weave intricate patterns through the crowd, the crowd who fell into step with them, repeating their motions and path exactly in a lagging train. 'That's my Amy!' said a voice beside him, and Mr. Raddlescott recognised the insolent baker from behind his ursid mask. 'Amy! It's me! Come home, Amy! Come home!' but the girl's horned-owl mask betrayed no recognition, fixated with ritual intensity upon leading the dance. Moaning quietly to himself, the baker slipped into their midst, jigging as though baited by invisible hounds and pikestaffs. Soon he was lost in the sweltering train that the dancers were leading around the tent like a great puppet dragon. Mr. Raddlescott's head was beginning to swim. He felt thirsty and nauseous. Colours and shapes were starting to blur and merge together; each movement of the chaotic dance was multiplied by an array of chromatic fires. He couldn't tell villagers from Turanians, let alone discern Lucian through the mad morass. Somehow or other he too had begun to dance, with heavy footfalls and sharp raking breaths, the rough inner surface of the mask chafing against the bridge of his nose. The strange, visceral music rose and fell, somehow more within him than without, swelling with coarse charisma. He was exhausted, and had at no point consciously desired to join in the revelries – but still he kept dancing, huffing and stamping through the horde of masked phantoms. Somehow now they seemed more fully to embody their animal disguises – their movements disinhibited, their identities forsaken, their passions writ more plainly on exhausted bodies than was possible on naked faces. They had descended into ecstasy – and he had joined them.

At some hidden signal the great carnival dissolved, and dilating into a circular formation its supplicants collapsed in panting heaps. The grassy ground had been almost entirely upturned by the churn of dancing feet. Turanians walked among the herd in gorgeous tasselled gowns of many silks and colours. In his strange delirium, Mr. Raddlescott was only mildly surprised to see them pulling beautiful languorous serpents out of great patchwork bags, and passing them among the crowd. Entirely docile, they let themselves be draped across many laps, and tickled beneath their scaly chins. A rancid condensation of drool and spiced breath and Kykeon froth had formed in the mask around Mr. Raddlescott's mouth, but somehow he felt unable to take it off. Everyone else had theirs firmly affixed. He was bound to it, somehow – and with this thought, he felt the old panic rising: the old tyranny of material objects. He watched a horse and a lion carry a carved wooden seat to the centre of the circle, and powerless to escape, watched them slowly approach him. They gently helped him to his feet and guided him to the chair, where he sat down heavily. His respectable coat was ripped and frayed. 'Supplicants!' cried the horse, 'our guest of honour!' And amongst the masses, the chant began to rise. Slowly at first, but soon it was as hypnotic as the thrum of Turanian zithers: 'Zagreus! Zagreus! Zagreus!' 'The god is within him!' the lion was crying, while the goat who had acted as the as gatekeeper of the Fête had emerged to wrap a golden robe around Mr. Raddlescott's shoulders. He wound a crown of ivy about his horns, and placed a wand of fennel in his hand. From the depths of hallucination, he began to protest – 'the tyranny! The tyranny of material things!' when the goat put a comforting hand on his shoulder. 'We are here to release you from all tyranny', he spoke in a silken voice, 'do not fear'. And then the sacrifice was brought.

Four robed Turanians bore him to the wooden throne. The crowd began once more to chatter and chant in excitement. 'The god must strike the first blow' the lion was roaring, 'before we can all join spirits in the ecstasy of Sparagmos!' a mighty cheer rang out. 'Just as the Titans once dismembered mighty Zagreus, may our sacrifice be sundered limb from limb!' The crowd knew exactly what to expect. 'Zagreus! Zagreus! Zagreus!' they raved in unison. The vessel of the god stood up and looked inquisitively at the sacrifice elect. He was wearing the mask of a monkey, and for a moment Mr.

Raddlescott thought he recognised the eyes behind it. 'Lucian?' he asked aloud in wonder. 'Why did you trade me away, dad?' the boy seemed to ask, 'how could you get rid of me like just another material thing?' 'I didn't mean that-' said the god incarnate, 'how could you do such a thing? How could you be such a tyrant to your son?' asked his sacrifice. Now Mr. Raddlescott clenched his teeth in rage. 'You are my son and for that I will always love you. But you are a fool… and for that I will tan your foolish hide'. He raised his hand. The crowd cheered in frenzy. The sacrifice looked up at him with pleading eyes – and before the blow could fall, twisted free from its captors and scampered away on its knuckles, hooting mischievously. The crowd erupted into a chorus of laughter while Mr. Raddlescott sat down, cradling his crowned mask in disorientation. Mister Wrinkles had vanished into the masses. Even the Turanians were laughing at this unusual turn of events. The only person at the Fête who didn't find it remotely comical was Zagreus himself.

But the momentum had risen, and the ceremonies proceeded as if guided by a hidden hand. 'The vessel shall mount his holy chariot', intoned the Turanians, 'and descend like mighty Zagreus of old!' At once, a troop of painted boys put their torches to scented braziers, and the great pillar in the centre of the big top – which Mr. Raddlescott had so far barely noticed, having assumed it was a structural support – blazed brightly with sacral flame. It seemed to him an enormous tree, sprawling and beautiful, reaching high into the shadows and trellised with ivy in a magnificent twisting scaffold. The Turanians walked with him in procession. As he ascended, he grew slowly less and less aware of the crowd cheering and howling below, and more intensely aware of his journey: ascending the world-tree with his animal guides, this strange axis mundi whose creaking boughs held up the patched and motley firmament. Alarmingly, he was beginning to think in metaphors – it was the influence of this fantastical atmosphere, perhaps, or the Turanians' visionary brew – or of Zagreus himself. So high above the ground, he felt the presence of the god with a strange intensity. He had almost forgotten why he had come here. 'The god will mount his chariot!' cried the goat-man, while the horse and lion showed Mr. Raddlescott to its gleaming car, nestled amongst the topmost boughs of the great nodding tree. He was tired from the climb and sat down with relief; his head still spinning with rich scents and colours and even ideas. The universe seemed so strange and full of mystery. The material world seemed pale and insignificant – and somehow Zagreus knew that it would never trouble him again. He took the reins, which were sharp as steel cable. 'And now the god will descend to the underworld' said the goat-man with joy, as he pulled the lever.

***

Reclining outside in his caravan, Lucian Raddlescott heard an almighty crash, followed by a mad ecstasy of cheering, laughing, screaming from inside the big top. It only diverted his attention briefly. He turned back to the book the Turanian had given him, spiced maroon leather with gilt Morocco binding. A thing of utter beauty. 'In theatres of antiquity' he read, 'actors would be artificially lowered from a height above the stage to resolve impossible dilemmas. This practise was referred to as God from the Machine'. He pondered this for a moment, and deliciously turned another page.

# THE MAIDEN OF THE MOSS

Words, I have often considered, possess an extraordinary similitude with the order *Coleoptera*. And just as the Creator might nurture an inordinate fondness for beetles, so, at risk of hubris, do we lesser poets exalt in the nigh-infinite number and variety of words. It pains me to admit that most words, like most beetles, will forever go unseen and unknown to common folk – and that the majority of each serve not the faintest human interest. But their beauty is quite undeniable.

Perhaps the most beautiful thing I have ever seen was a display of *Coleoptera* under glass in the old Faculty museum, gleaming like the jewels of some mediaeval Hereafter – although beauty is perhaps the wrong term for it. It was instead, I suppose, handsome in the manner of an old lexicon: attractively frownish with authority, the dignity and permanence of an honourable old headstone. But I desiderate the life of things. To see those same multitudes shuffling their gauzy skirts beneath enamel breastplates, shimmering like oils in a sorcerer's alembic – now there is a beauty! It was the beauty which drew me away from the pinboard of entomology and into the vibrant life of words, and I have come to suspect that it is a sort of beauty endemic only to a living language; a language that flows from the nib of the tongue like a butterfly miraculous from its jar of ether. And it is this language that I have come to seek, like any worthwhile searcher after specimens, in my walks through the forest.

If a poem is like a walk, as I have heard it described, then a novel is surely like the forest. To read is to create a 'desire path'. And the way in which each reader chooses to disturb the understory of this forest (you shall pardon the pun) is in itself a most fascinating under-story. I blunt my quill on this matter for a simple reason. For the forest in which I took my customary strolls very much resembled the setting of my first novel – quite accidentally, my first bestseller – *Lampyris*. 'They had been as two fireflies, each chasing the other's lantern in a dizzy ring. But now their wicks were running short, and the circular haste to catch the other was slowly becoming a haste to escape'. I do fear I shall live to see it in the 'classics' section. To the great delight of my old publishers, the follow-up, *Hob-Owls in Gloaming*, was finished the very next year – released to a public whose appetite for the works of Baird O. Fenimore (I have never had cause for a *nom de plume*) was understandably at its crest. Sales were perplexingly high – and it even made the lists (to my horrified chagrin) across the pond. But interest tapered quickly; helped, in no small measure, by the reviews. A sincere shame, it was generally felt, for a young author (I was forty-three) to prostitute his artistry after such an unusual and promising debut. They weren't entirely wrong – and after one too many disreputable comparisons with the prose of *Woodland Magazine* (of all things), I quite freely admit the error of my opportunism. Nonetheless, *Lampyris* was still paying for my daily crusts, my reputation was young and my imagination was correspondingly supple. The greatest thing, I thought, to kickstart my literary convalescence, would be to write another book. A redemption story, as it were – a recapturing of that magical lamplight that flooded out of bookshops only half a misty decade ago. And I have gotten absolutely nowhere.

In a less figurative sense, I suppose, I have indeed gotten 'somewhere' – and that somewhere is a little cottage at the bottom of the river Torrill, whose back garden blends delightfully in with those twenty private acres of broadleaf forest where she and I are both wont to perambulate along a rather impressive gorge. With the fulcrum of her latest 'adventure' with a city poet (who had been, but aren't they all, some sort of deconstructionist), it had been easy enough to tilt things in my favour with Annis, who had assented to the move – 'if it would really bring me another bestseller'. The cottage is, theoretically, a place highly conducive to my craft. We lived off our savings, and the royalties of my surprising breakthrough. And every day I packed my notebook and my thermos for a walk through the forest, hoping at last to forage the right language for my heretofore most slow and troublesome return to the bookshelves.

One of my favourite reviews of *Lampyris* had commented (with an awe only partially misplaced) on 'Fenimore's uncommon faculty for seeing beneath the experiential dross of things'. And while the same reviewer subsequently found my authorly vision bleared by 'that impenetrable *Gloaming*', it was precisely this faculty that my walks along the little gorge of the Torrill were poised to stimulate. It always began with a deep green feeling – gold light through slender sprigs of late summer, picking out details with the forgivable overenthusiasm of a young artist rightfully certain of success. Past the lip of envy, I became conscious of the 'glitter' – the tiny speckles of spray thrown up by the Torrill as she cut her way down through chalky under-layers or riffled around boulders. I only half-believed in this 'glitter': the tiny dusting of visual icing-sugar that made the forest so much sweeter, as if each infinitesimal drop was throwing out a homeopathic dose of rainbow, and decocting pigments ground from heavenly cochineal into the palette of that enviable young painter. Now there's a sentence that wouldn't have floated with my old editors. But it is a *living* sentence, that could only have been born here in the forest, on the high banks of the Torrill. So what if her rapids tinkled like the harps of elfland? If her song suggested the wise, pacific syllables of 'susurrus' or 'murmur?' There was no deadening sentimentality to these thoughts – no cynical undercurrent, no chance for a deadening footnote to dangle off the paragraph's ankle like a ball-and-chain. I drew a glittering breath. It was my inspiration.

Truth to tell, the exercise of these mental meanderings was a daily relief. I still had it in me, somewhere – that commended ability to see the seeds of art in life. It's why I left my job studying insects, which was really a job testing pesticides. The magnifying glass kept turning into a picture frame, which was a metaphor quite central to *Lampyris*, a work (rather predictably) concerned with the properties and symbolism of light. I have come to pretend that *Hob-Owls in Gloaming* was about darkness, but really of course it was about money. And as for my next book – after years of false-starting – I was only now beginning to get an idea of what *it* was going to be about. The right language was forming with every walk I took through the forest. It had just taken a very long time to grow.

The story, of course, wouldn't just be about the forest. I rather suspect I have expended the goodwill of my readers on that theme already. Nor would it be, much as her whispering passage enchanted me endlessly, *entirely* about the river – although she had at least earned her rightful place in the dedication. Our flows had become inseparable. There is an oft-remarked similitude between the waters and the mind, where life rises from one as ideas from the other. What, then, I ponder as I make it, is the import of taking a walk upstream? There's more to it than watching water-beetles whirling in still pools. There's surely something mythic in the journey, in following the river to its spring in the heart of the forest. There's a mystery inherent in tracing things back to their sources. The eternal myth of origins, and a rare poetry in the fact that the source of my ideas coincided so neatly with that of the river. Torrill's glamour glazed the whole forest with vibrance, painted reflections on every leaf and rubbed rouge on every mushroom-cup. Her vital element dusted my brow and my cheeks. These were adjectives and adverbs of the language of life; a language composed of infinitely subtler composites than that tedious textbook, deoxyribonucleic acid. I understood in those walks something of how the heroes of ancient song had their beauties gilded by the goddess. It was a matter of description. The further I walked up the curving gorge of the river, the further I came to an understanding of the language of life – and how better, I thought, to escape the underworld of my literary infamy.

The forest deepened with Torrill's gorge, and I put my hands to my shoulder-straps, the hiker's salute unto awe. The air was rich with vapour and glittered like mica; the woods drank it with glee. Stems like fluted glasses, flowerbuds like tight bunches of grapes, each leaf itself a canopy to shade some couch of fey repose. Torrill's muted tirra-lirra; froth hissing on husky gravel, growing still more muted as I mounted at last that hillock, her cradle. Torrill's voice mewed softly from the earth, tinkling, tweeting over green stones. I had made good time.

I rested against the squat stone of the little hill and drank my tea, tracing the sprawl of a great grandfather oak from tip to trunk, like tributaries on a floodplain, like nervous threads. It was a calming exercise, to move one's eyes along those streams, and I found myself doing it often – even without the tutelary presence of the bosky sage; even at home, when I shut my eyelids and released my mind in moments before sleep. The tea was warm and misted in the spray. Torrill splashed about the stones. Splash, wash, gush; arbitrariness principle be damned, these were loan-words from the language of life! And here, upon my hillock in the heart of the forest, I had come into the presence of perhaps its most fluent speaker. Not Torrill herself, indeed – part of me feels that the language is too close a quality of her being for fair comparison. I speak instead of the moss. Moss everywhere like fine, green dust. Furring the stones, the hill, the beardy trunks of oaken sprawl, as if each drop of vapour was a tiny seed, in whose crystal pod curls a forest fibre, which finally settling unfolds and entwines with its thousand-thousand neighbours into a woven raiment for the undergrowth. It is greener than grass, for it occupies the negative space between the blades, and ever more in-between, like the florets of the Roman cauliflower. Linkages and ligatures in layers, endless gradients of green whose depth and density must go forever unproven by human tongues and fingers. But we may listen. I conjugate my ear to the mossy stone. Just beyond the bridge of my nose, a tiny beetle with a yellow bean for an abdomen interprets her way through the lattice. I close my eyes.

There are a pair of mycological concepts which often return to me during my meditations in this part of the forest, both related, incidentally, to the formation of faerie-rings. The first is the 'necrotic zone'. Sometimes the subterraneous fungal networks which coalesce to form faerie-rings secrete chemicals that compromise the growth of surface plantlife, or elsewise outcompete them. The result is a glyph of desolation upon the landscape which superstitions of old came, perhaps reasonably, to distrust or despise – here the devil set his milk-churn, here the witch scorched a sigil for some dark perverted mass. And yet some of these mycorrhizal systems nurture where others strangle. They release substances which act like developmental hormones for the surrounding vegetation, and so form a 'rapid growth zone'. Instead of an earthen scar, the meadow is marked with exuberant patterns of flourishing – here the auld folk dance by moonlight, here protrude the steeple-tops of a faerie hamlet, et cetera, et cetera. But the fact that such antithetical phenomena occur in the same circular forms, and maybe even consecutively (or so I like to imagine) in the same faerie-ring, strikes me as deeply poetic. There are times when I consider the mossy hillock in the heart of the forest to be one such zone of rapid growth, and think, beneath the shaggy stones and vertigoes of deepening green, what is the substratum of this life; what sacred truffle pulsates in unquiet death beneath the stones, pumping moss and ferns and beetles upwards? And then I hear the river Torrill, softly, sweetly, slithering from the earth, sketching her first tentative attempts at a gorge. She is a primitive stonemason with a wedge of blunt antler-bone and a maul of gravity. The god of carving is always a god of water. This is no hillock, but a barrow, the tomb of an ancient priestess, an ancient healer; the tomb of Torrill, the maiden of the moss, who makes all things green and whisper…

*The Maiden of the Moss…*

It would serve for a title.

I opened my eyes to see the sun, a phoenix-nest in the arms of the ancient oak. My ear was still pressed to the moss, and my reverie was that of a castaway sunk in foam. I stuck my tongue out and drank a dewdrop from the fronds. *The Maiden of the Moss.* Yes, it would serve. She was still talking to me. Insects chirruped deep inside the spongy pith of the moss. The wind played the bones on the branches, a warbler rang the tiny bell in its throat, a quartet of early crickets spluttered like fat squibs of saltpetre and haemolymph. And as I wrote down my thoughts in the notebook, I felt like I was talking back to her. To see is to be seen, I thought, to touch is to be touched, I was an infant, learning to grow old by language. When the sun had fallen low enough, I lifted my head from the stone. For a few seconds the inverted topography of my outer ear lingered in the dense moss. I watched it melt into the landscape, quick as snow. I felt like King Arthur, feeling the bruised stalks of that grassy impress where, for a single night and never again, the queen of faeries had lain by his side.

\*\*\*

I returned then into the breadbox warmth of the cottage. I closed the door and the whispers of the river became a faint static. My boots seemed to 'clob clob' with uncomfortable loudness as I wiped them off on the doormat: 'welcome', and scraped them off my thermal-stockinged feet. The scratch of nylon as my windbreaker went up on the peg and I padded into the kitchen. 'Hey, Annis', I called, and heard a cup hit the sink. My dear old Mrs. Fenimore was staring at the washing-up in a woolly orange jumper. A twinge of regret. 'I'm bloody cold' she said. 'Tea?' I offered, and she shot back a unilateral look. 'And bloody tired. You're back late'. 'Well, I'm – not really'. I went to put the kettle on. 'I took a hike into the village this morning'. She said. 'Oh? Did you say you were going to get-' 'No. I just had to go. Cold meats tonight. I've had soup'. 'Right, okay, that's okay, sorry I was late'. I remembered I had left my thermos in the bag. It needed to be washed or else the 'stainless steel' would contradict itself to disastrous effect – but now wasn't the time. Mrs. Fenimore looked at me lean and hard. 'Did you get any work done?' She asked. The question was not bitter, not exactly – but it had become phatic. It had meant something to her, a few years ago – and now it meant something to me. Something different. The water had boiled but I didn't move. 'Well, I suppose I have', I said. 'That's lovely, darling'. 'No, no, really I have!'

I suddenly realised that I had boiled the kettle without tea – or a mug – at the ready. I opened the cupboard – 'tea?' I offered, and bit my tongue. Annis raised her eyebrow. 'You've already asked. Have you been listening to me?' 'Annis, I meant – you said you were-', 'cold yes, distant too, perhaps: tomorrow I shall go into town for a nylon windbreaker to keep me warm while I gather flowers all day and toss the basket in the river on my way home. Where are my flowers, Baird? Why the hell did we move here if you aren't putting together a bloody bouquet? You know it can't last.' 'What?' 'Oh bloody hell, what. I'm wasting my life out here – we're wasting our lives. It makes me feel so old having nothing to do – and when you come back from your daily frisks with nothing to show for it, it makes me feel bloody *ancient*. I'm cold and bloody tired'. Her tone became

grave. 'You should go back to the lab'. 'The lab, but –
Annis, I'm an *author*! I hate death – I hate pesticides
– I hate...' 'What did you say?' 'I said-' 'Pests, you
said, pests inside, now which pests do you mean
exactly?' 'No, that's not what I-' 'Oh, isn't it? Is that
what you think I do all day? Roaching around while
you're off gallivanting, weaving a daisy-chain for the
garden gnome and forgetting your bloody notebook
on the bedside table.' 'I didn't-' 'I can't believe we
sold the motor'. 'Well, we needed-' 'Baird. Listen to
me. There's just *no progress*!' And she walked out of
the kitchen, leaving me to choke.

Later I heard her talking on the telephone.
No progress. I am Penelope. I weave all day, and
every night I unravel that which I have wrought in
thread, in linkage and ligament, in language. Perhaps
*The Necrotic Zone* would be a better title. Perhaps
not. I am unravelling as we speak, denaturing,
declining into a skein of second thoughts. She's in the
sitting room, laughing on the telephone, closing all
the windows I opened because she's cold, and when
they're closed, she opens them because it's stifling,
and I am at the root of it because 'all this was for me'.
I'm alone in the bedroom. The moon shines through
scratches in the glass. The mattress is a pale blue
desert, creased with dunes. I close my eyes and try to
trace the wild gesticulations of the shaman oak, but
my eyes grow weary with meandering nowhere

beneath their lids. Torrill rushes faintly outside but it is not enough to make me remember the sound of her voice, the lilting forms of her strange, pure words. Every day I learn to speak anew, and every night I am made mute again, and it is little wonder I have not been able to write. A copy of *Hob-Owls in Gloaming* lies on the bedside table, spine unwrinkled: above it, a handbook of feng shui, lovingly thumbed. I have forgotten to wash-up the thermos flask.

\*\*\*

Annis didn't talk to me in the morning. Her crumpled blankets and hot water bottle were still on the sofa when I left for the woods. The Maiden of the Moss was waiting for me, waiting once again to distil her sweet pure hippocrene. This time, I thought, I would not betray her. This time I would not let her words go forgotten. I took a small trowel with me from the garden.

'What have you done to the bonsai tree?' Annis asked me that evening. She had put down the phone and was staring at me from the sitting room. I was working away at my notes on the kitchen table. 'Sorry?' 'I said, why have you been tampering with my bonsai tree?' The tree in question was stood on the mantlepiece. It had been a gift from an admirer, and though I liked it better than the other absurd and lifeless objects that littered the cottage for the purposes of 'channelling flow', it had always struck me as painfully superfluous when one might simply open the window and feel a flow of such indefinitely superior intensity. 'You haven't trimmed it in a while' I said, not answering the question. Annis kept staring. 'What? I've only transplanted a bit of moss. Put a bit of life back into the old fellow. Connect him to his local environment maybe. Have you seen the moss outside, Annis? It's really beautiful stuff'.

She buried her head in her hands. I think perhaps she even laughed – an unpleasant sound, halfway to a sob. It was a lost cause laugh. 'I can't believe we're actually gathering moss, Baird. We're *gathering moss* here'. I stopped my writing. 'I really think it's quite beautiful though. Look at the colour.' 'No, you didn't hear me. I said we're gathering moss here. We're literally *gathering moss*, Baird. We're *literally gathering-*' 'I heard you.' 'No. You're not hearing me. I *said-*' 'No, I heard you!' 'No!'

I closed my notebook, hoping to protect the day's work from doubt, from forgetting, from the pen which stood cocked in my own mute and mutinous hand. 'I've just put a bit of moss in with the houseplants, Annis. It's not symbolic, alright? It's just nice'. Her head remained in her hands for a long time. Her shoulders rose and fell in hills of orange woolly jumper, whether in laughing, crying, breathing, I cannot say. And then she got up and closed the window. But this time I could open my notebook. And I wrote; wrote half-remembered words in a language which had for the first time survived the daily glossectomy of the home. I had begun to create *The Maiden of the Moss*.

The next day I scooped up some stones from Torrill's banks, filled the empty flowerpots in the garden, and smothered them in soil and growing moss from the hillock. The maiden of the moss had never been more communicative. I could hear her whisper now even in the cottage, drowning out the deafening silence of the telephone over which Annis spent ever more time talking, laughing, crying, breathing. The moss was green and lush, I kept it moist and glittering with a spray-bottle of river water, and it grew with unbelievable fullness, almost to radiance. If I put my ear to it, I could really hear the quickening tongue; the faint chittering of tiny things, the rich scent and heritage of wet and mud. I recorded it all.

'Pests inside, pests inside, pests inside' mumbled Annis. I had actually just finished drafting the first chapter of *The Maiden of the Moss* when the beetles hatched. Tiny, ravenous little weevils with wing-cases the colour of mustard and butterbeans; they came from the moss in great numbers, I must have brought them in from the forest. They were beautiful. Water dewed their tiny thighs like studs of diamond, and when they burrowed out from beneath the blanketing green, it was *Lampyris* anew: 'as if the ground had opened those eyes which once belonged alone to the sky at night'. Annis stared at the bonsai tree they had used for their food, its trunk bored through with a million miniscule drills, its fibres mulched into wattle for those quaint dwellings the old wives once likened to the boots of faerie-folk. 'Pests inside, pests inside, pests inside...' she mumbled to herself, blanketed on the sofa, as the beetles began to whet their tiny mandibles on the wooden beams, the skirting boards, the legs of our few antique chairs. Annis had, curiously enough, begun to cultivate the moss. When I returned home from Torrill's tomb one day, I found that she had planted moss in all the empty flowerpots in the garden, and she laughed when I asked her about it, and I laughed in response, because it was all so beautiful, and I was overjoyed that she had joined me in celebrating so fluent an interlocutor. That this invitation extended to an entourage of beetles, liveried in sulphur, was a meagre price: though like Lear's knights they quaffed and gorged amid the woodwork, their presence was welcome, for they spoke the language with a rare, low dialect, and it was very pleasing to the ear and so very useful for the book.

Another day I came home to see that the moss had overrun the lips of each flowerpot, and like the shorn fur of some exquisite jungle beast, was oozing along the cracks in the flagstones and into the bristles of the doormat: 'we come'. The paint on the door had begun to peel like stripped hangnails, revealing pock-riddled planks whose damp rifts were already colonised with tufted green. Inside, rainwater dripped from the ceiling. I stuck my tongue out to catch it. So refreshing. Moss had overrun the floorboards, the walls, the sunken, ruined furniture, caking the closed windows, blooming from the telephone receiver like hairs in an elderly ear. I put down my notebook on what remained of a coffee table. The ground was spongy beneath my boots, our rugs had reverted half to earth, and the sitting room had become a crawling vivarium, a pocket ecosystem of moss and mould and tiny weevils like yellow grains, weevils whose taxonomy eluded me because I had ceased to concern myself with such trivialities, and because the angular structures of Latin were offensive in comparison to the beautiful language of life which dripped and oozed and chirruped and thundered distantly through gorges in the woods, and through moss so matted that it might have grown nourished on the chin of a waterfall.

And then the moss began to move, shifting on the moist and sagging mass which I now perceived had once been the sofa. She was there, her limbs curled tight as those of a sapling yet to germinate, whispering softly beneath a blanket that had resolved into moss on both sides. I went to her, and tried gently to peel it back, but found I could not, for it had fused. Life had become interleaved. Her orange woolly jumper was rotten and radiant with bright green moss. It fixed in her straggled hair like clumps of fungus. It worked its wondrous tapestry like a chrysalis over her pale skin; rooting moss in the caves of her collarbone, in the corners of her twitching mouth, in her nostrils, in her ears. *The Maiden of the Moss.* I kissed her. She unwove a frail arm and pulled me closer, putting her pallid lips to my ear; those lips which had tasted like the dew on the barrow, tasted like the river Torrill.

And she whispered words to me in a language I could not understand. It wasn't a language of words and letters and literature. It was the language of life, and it sounded like silence, for it could not be expressed. It is a language only suggested in the soft chittering of a million tiny beetles, forever crawling and clicking through the undergrowth of perception, who even now were beginning to write the book that none could have written by turning its fibres to pulp and nutriment for a million tiny mouths.

# EXPEDITION OF THE *RONNOCH MOR*

Captain Swope had passed away in the storm. He had been out on the deck trying to fix down the towing warps when he had collapsed, fracturing the base of his skull. Dr. Whelan said that his death had been instantaneous.

Captain Swope had been a seasoned fisherman, but he was old, and ever since the heart attack he had suffered – a grim portent – on the *Ronnoch Mor's* previous expedition, there had been reason to question his robustness. Dr. Whelan, who had chartered the captain's seventy-five foot stern trawler for both voyages, had been closest to him. He knew that his wife had been concerned for his health during this voyage – and now there was no way, for better or worse, to assuage her concern. The storm had utterly hamstrung the *Ronnoch Mor*'s wheelhouse – communications were down, as were echosounders and assisted navigation. Its systems were much too finely fangled for Sermon, the crew's sole and silent engineer, to revive, although to his credit the Diesel, which we feared might also have been waterlogged, was in perfect order. Pressed to our cotsides, listening to the creaking of cables and the clanking of the crane, none could tell how long the squall had lasted. Through the porthole it was almost painterly. The weather was so excessive as to seem unchanging, fixed in a moment of ectopic pregnancy. When normality finally came, it came oozing from the tumult like a creature from its crumpled eggshell. It was a clam-diver ascending from the bays of remote antiquity, dribbling rich green oil. The *Ronnoch Mor* was adrift, somewhere in the North Sea, with no land in sight, no communications, and no captain.

We had been reduced to a crew of four. Dr. Elson Whelan was, in the absence of Captain Swope, its most senior member – and it was for the purposes of his research that the *Ronnoch Mor* had been chartered for its second expedition. Both Sermon and Groff, the deckhand, had worked with Dr. Whelan on a previous collecting trip, surveying the littoral biota along the western coast of Norway and into circumpolar waters. The trip had been successful, by all accounts: they had discovered twelve new invertebrate species, one of which, a sort of pelagic shrimp, had since been identified as a commercially viable source of protein by the Department of Fisheries. But it had not been so successful as to rule out a second voyage. For one thing, Dr. Whelan explained, they had no proper way to record the living qualities of the creatures they dredged up – ethological factors were important for classification, and even such basic identifiers as colour were quickly lost in the process of preservation. I had been hired as the ship's photographer. Each time the trawl was winched aboard to spill its bounty upon the white enamel sorting-tray, I would be poised with my trusty thirty-five millimetre to record those vital colours which, in aesthetics and cladistics both, divided the mundane from the novel. I had my developing tank and chemicals in the hold, where we stored the biological samples once they had been jarred, labelled, and steeped in formaldehyde. I had brought enough film to last for six weeks, the planned length of the scientific expedition. And now that plan appeared distressingly uncertain.

I was in favour of giving Captain Swope a seaman's burial, with a tarp for his winding-sheet and a weight for his headstone. A noble interment, and one, I think, he would have appreciated, but one – as Dr. Whelan reasoned – that would be hard on his poor wife. The *Ronnoch Mor* was not large enough to possess a freezer room for fish-packing, which grievously narrowed our options. Groff brought up the story of some famous admiral who, having died at sea, was kept by his crew in a barrel of wine – and though our own rations of such life-affirming stuff had dwindled considerably during the storm, the *Ronnoch Mor*'s supply of life-preserving alternatives did not long escape notice. And what was more, noted Dr. Whelan, following a memorable failure of the last collecting trip (whereby what was almost certainly a new species of crab had to be discarded on account of its being simply too large to preserve) – he had invested in a hundred-gallon tub, complete with glass lid and windows for observation, which at this very moment was standing vacant in the hold. I wish I had mustered the courage to protest. It didn't seem right to pickle an experienced seaman like just another rarity from the deep. But my misgivings, of course, were quickly overruled. Sermon and Groff stripped Captain Swope of his oilfrock while I grudgingly filled the tub with formaldehyde, a rag tied around my mouth and nose. They bore the body, mummified in thermal underclothes, into the darkness of the trawler's hold. Dr. Whelan said a few words, and then the captain was unceremoniously embalmed. I shuddered at the scraping of the glass observation panel. Pale, labelled things would hold his wake, packed around the tub in silent choruses. And his colours would begin to leach – and he would slowly die again, fading like a hesitant spectre.

Do not mistake my uneasiness for disrespect, or, worse, contempt for my crewmates. With no certain rescue in sight, there was little room for such enmities. It arises merely from an instinct – ironically – of self-preservation. I have always sought to distance myself from death. Some of my earliest memories are those of rifling through albums of family photographs, asking my father for names of people I would never see, hearing his voice crack as my little finger paused over a portrait of a young woman and he made the answer: 'that was your mother'. I have always had a rather sensitive, some might say squeamish, disposition, and mastering the camera was my method of coping with a sort of weakness. It made it remarkably easy to abstract an image from reality, to make it small; something you can hold, collect, fold, throw away. Photography is war against death. And at heart I was discomforted to know that the only place on the trawler that was dark enough to develop my photographs was the place I would have to share henceforth with a permanent reminder of human mortality. The racks and rows of biological samples had been unsettling enough, but they could be tolerated because I had taken their photographs while they still squirmed on a field of white enamel in an inch of seawater – and so saved something of their spirits from the ghastly creeping pallor of the jars. But a human being… now that was surely something different.

Soon afterwards Dr. Whelan summoned us up to the foredeck. He had unlocked the captain's cabin to return the dead man's possessions – and there discovered a flare gun. In its chipped red case were stashed three flares. 'Whoever's on watch', he said, 'especially at night, must keep the flare gun close'. Murmurs of assent from Groff and a nod from Sermon. 'If you see a vessel – any vessel – pop one into the sky and call the rest of us. Only one, mind'. He paused grimly. 'Later attempts may be necessary'.

It had been three days since the storm had passed, and two since we had put the captain in the hold. The atmosphere was strange. We had somehow skipped the panic of being set adrift – or rather, perhaps, exhausted it prematurely in the who-knows-how-long of the storm itself. Dr. Whelan was doing a fair job of keeping the crew together, although he too was somewhat out of his element, and had never struck me as a natural leader. The absence of the captain above decks was as conspicuous as his presence below. And the mood was sombre, almost pensive – helped in no small measure by the aftermath of the tempest. The sea was grey-green and weirdly flat, the waves like teeth too small for a smile, and the sky seemed uncomfortably low; uncomfortably thick with a mat of milky cloud which stretched as far as the eye could see. Wispy fibres crisscrossed like fishbones in an owl pellet. It was a sky as stifling as cotton wool. And it diffused the light in such a peculiar manner that one couldn't quite tell with exactitude where the sun rose and where it would set. Groff, who had picked up some navigation in his years as a deckhand, was concerned to discover that the thick web of cloud admitted not the merest glimmer of starlight. And I was afraid that the bizarre, dead, omnivalent filtration of the light would have some adverse effect on my photography. It was difficult enough having to account for subjects immersed in two fingerwidths of water under normal illumination, let alone in this claustral purgatory. Everything seemed close, flat, mid-tonal; everything seemed somehow less *there* for want of its natural shadow and hue.

Dr. Whelan was insistent that we keep a tight ship, and keep ourselves sane by sticking to routine and ritual as closely as we could until some help arrived, or the skies cleared enough for Groff to try his hand at the captain's charts. That meant, he smiled, that we should make the most of our unfortunate circumstances, and that specimen collection would continue as planned. There was little else that could be done. Myself and the deckhand, under Whelan's supervision, were set to preparing the bottom trawl. It was a sizeable construction with a robust footrope, nine feet across, alternately weighted with lead bobbins and set with the decapitated medusae of old mops. 'To sweep up or entangle smaller specimens', the scientist explained, although to my elementary knowledge of trawling it wasn't that much of an explanation. They had done it, or so he claimed, on the *Challenger* – and so it was worth emulating. The otter boards were like steel ploughshares, hydrodynamic enough to preserve the *Ronnoch Mor*'s engine as she dragged the trawl along the seafloor. The net itself was long and conical, the cod-end with a custom weave whose mesh was illegally fine for commercial use – but perfectly within limits, we were assured, for our present purposes of scientific exploration. The *Ronnoch Mor* was a stern trawler, so there was none of the usual fussing with booms and beams. Once the headrope was fitted with a few additional floaters to maintain a wide gape, and the construction itself was hooked securely to the warp of the aft-winch, the trawling could begin. The doctor called Sermon, who took his place in the wheelhouse, and set the ship going at a pace of four knots. We watched the trawl darken as the slate grey seas consumed it. The winch wailed as the towing warp unravelled. We had three thousand feet of cable, at least a thousand of which would be superfluous wherever we happened to be, and a red band marked its unspooling every hundred feet: now two hundred, now three hundred, now four. The trawl seemed to settle somewhere above four hundred feet; we estimated just below seventy-five fathoms.

The deckhand raised his gravelly voice. He was young, but he had taken up the maritime life to escape a loveless family, and the nautical miles and salt and smoke had aged him like cod. 'Seventy-five fathoms. Can we check the cap's charts and see where we might be drifting?'. Dr. Whelan did not need to be asked twice. But he returned with his head shaking sorrowfully. 'We could be more or less anywhere, Groff. We can only rule out Dogger Bank'. 'Our waters?' 'Yes. But it is much shallower than this. It's thought it used to be a land bridge, you know, connecting Britain to the continent. Captain Swope once told me about a Danish trawler which pulled up bits of tree and even an old arrowhead in a clump of peat. It's a strange thing. But it's not here, and it doesn't concern us'. And the *Ronnoch Mor* trudged on through the grey nothing, like a beggar hauling his heavy knapsack through snow.

At last Dr. Whelan ordered the trawl raised. All four of us gathered at the capstan and, with the *Ronnoch Mor* at anchor, began to haul. Even with four backs bent – mine by far the frailest – the ascent was painstaking. The capstan had a locking mechanism which was used precisely once to afford time to pass around a canteen of water, and of which I was much too cowardly to request any subsequent employments. I saw the crucifix tattooed on Sermon's stubbly throat bob up and down as he silently drank his share of the canteen. 'Perhaps we've over-weighted', said Dr. Whelan. 'Or perhaps', said Groff, 'we've got something big'. Fatter and fatter grew the coils on the winch, until eventually the great gauzy bulk of the trawl could be seen beneath the surface. The scientist and the deckhand went to prepare the large enamel observation tray, fetch buckets of fresh water for rinsing the specimens, jars, labels and formaldehyde to store them, while Sermon went to the mast-crane and began to lift the heaving trawl amidships. I went to get my camera, noticing that it still contained a spool of partially undeveloped film.

With everyone in position, Dr. Whelan gave the word, and Sermon released the catch. Hundreds of young lanternfish and glass shrimp spilled out with clods of benthic mud, bound by the serpentine links of brittle-stars, ragged sponges and flat mudcrabs like skipping stones which picked their way through the slurry and nibbled daintily at detritus. Silty clams, pulled up by the churning of the trawl-doors, cairned up in their hundreds, and the mopheads crawled with clamworms and bright red ribbons of nereis. A huge flounder threshed wearily amid the slime; Sermon broke its skull with a hammer in quiet announcement that we would forego the tins at mess that evening. And all throughout Dr. Whelan was there in his oilskins and leather gauntlet, sifting through the briny morass, occasionally isolating a specimen in the smaller tray, observing it, identifying it, and eventually calling me over to fortify the photographic record. My concerns about the light proved more than warranted; sometimes when the subject was lively I could barely see it through the blur of the viewfinder, and many of the photographs I had assured Dr. Whelan were adequately taken were in fact complete and literal shots in the dark. The development of this reel, I thought, may have to meet with a few tactical accidents. I began to adjust the aperture, trying in vain to counteract the directionless dimness of the sky, when I heard the doctor's exclamation. 'By god!', he cried, then, gesturing wildly for space, 'Out of the way, Kenspeckle!' he shouted, 'out of my way'. I had a second at most to scurry from my place by the shallow viewing basin before the doctor had assumed it, and, with a plop, transferred the subject of his attention. The shouting had caught the attention of the deckhand, who had so far been occupied hucking bycatch over the gunwales. 'What's that, doc?' he said, pulling back his gutterfront sou'wester and letting it hang round his neck. I peered over Dr. Whelan's shoulder. He was looking intently at the specimen. 'What is it?'

'I'm not sure' he said. 'Some sort of lobe-fin. Looks almost like a lungfish, but they're freshwater creatures. Look at those fins! They're almost like little legs'. The small, dull organism was sitting mazedly at the bottom of the tray. It was not, to me, a particularly impressive thing. 'There's something of the mudskipper about it, no?' asked Dr. Whelan. 'Perhaps we've stumbled upon a Lazarus taxon. By god, what if! It was only a few years ago that *Coelacanth* came out of the West Indies – after sixty six million years of so-called extinction!' 'Shall I perhaps photograph it for you, Dr. Whelan?' I asked. 'Yes, yes, of course', he said, keeping his gaze fixed on the archaic little beast, not moving away from the basin. 'Would you look at that', he said, 'I believe I can discern a parietal eye. But yes, quickly and be done with it, Kenspeckle, I must preserve this one quickly or risk morphological distortion, pressure differences and all. I'm not fully certain but I think we've made a real discovery here'.

The creature seemed to pose somnolently as I fixed it in the focusing grid of my camera. Blast the clouds, I thought, what an awful day for photography – and then I thought that this same cursed half-light was probably the only light the little fish had ever seen. Its species, if the doctor's hunch was to be trusted, had been removed from the daylight for millions of years. I was suddenly struck with the strangest paranoia, as if, of the two of us, I was the anachronism. The camera and the creature exchanged a thousand-year stare. And then I took the photograph, stepped out of the way, and watched Dr. Whelan excitedly rinse his specimen under the gills and neatly drown it in preservative.

\*\*\*

That night I went down to the hold to develop the photographs, occupying much of the descent in trepidation as to whether I should salute the body of the captain. Don't be foolish, I told myself, it means nothing to him now, forget he's even there. I saluted the captain.

The hold is by far the closest place to a darkroom on the ship, but for the purpose of developing photographs *in situ* and securely I had contrived to add my own developing tank to the ship's inventory. This small drumlike vessel is capped with a double lid, the first tier of which is set with a funnel for the induction of developing agents, stop bath and stabiliser, and the second tier of which prevents all light from entering the tank. It is a convenient little device, but the removal of the film from its canister and its winding around the reel which exposes it to chemicals in the tank cannot, obviously, be done inside it: that part of the process still relies on the darkened room. I stopped the crack of light beneath the door with an old length of tarp, extracted my rag from my pocket and covered my face, not only in defence against the highly acidic photographic developer, but the ambient formaldehyde which no doubt suffused this room of biological samples, whose volatility I trusted little. And then I began the development. I cracked open the film canister with my penknife, and, muscle memory doing fine service despite the numbing effects of glove on finger and total darkness, summarily loaded it around the reel and slotted it into the development tank. Now I could turn on the small electric lantern by which Dr. Whelan inspected the docked samples. Next the chemical bath, developer, warmed and agitated gently over a period of five minutes counted in my head, then the fixer, and finally the stabiliser. I noticed, although I had just enough for my present purpose, that the bottle of stabiliser was running dangerously light – I would have to dig into my supplies and pray I had packed surplus. But finally the film was immersed, and shortly after released, rinsed, and patiently unspooled. Nothing worse than crimped film, I told myself, as the ribbon of thirty-six colour negatives slowly emerged. They would need to be left to dry – but I couldn't help myself, and having rinsed my funnels to prevent future contaminations, took the line of photographs into the light. I shivered and stopped myself from arraying them upon what was definitely not a glass counter-top.

The results were disappointing. Dismaying, even. Everything was painfully underexposed. That damn sky, I thought to myself, those bloody clouds – all my fiddling with the aperture had been for naught. The lanternfish – or maybe even the shadows of the lanternfish – looked about as identifiable as pale grey strings of cloud at night. Excruciatingly, the little lobe-fin which Dr. Whelan had been so enthusiastic about looked like little more than a pale white tuber. It was actually rather ghastly. To see these once-vital organisms as underexposed negatives – pallid smears against shadow, cadaverous as sunbleached driftwood, was to look upon the jars of preservative that surrounded me in the hold; those vampiric vessels which, filled only yesterday with life that writhed in toxic shock, had already begin to suck the colour from their victims. The negatives were as unbearably grotesque as the faded specimens. My eyes scanned the line of photographs further and further backwards, flickering with extreme brevity over each ghastly inversion of life and colour, until at last they came to the first picture of the reel – a picture which, I only now realised, had not been part of yesterday's batch. The film had not been a new one, I remembered, and I certainly hadn't been able to get the full thirty-six pictures from it yesterday. There were a few very poor images of the storm – looking, I noted with a certain dread, as pale and unwholesome as the blanket of low cloud it had pulled in from goodness-knows-where – but it was the very first picture on the film that gave me pause. It had been taken before the tempest. A colour negative of the *Ronnoch Mor*'s crew, arrayed in oilskins which were more the colour of labcoats. There was Groff, compact, lean, and looking into the distance, there was Sermon, as vocal as he was in life, staring straight into the camera. Dr. Whelan was there, smiling with his hands on the observation tray. And there was Captain Swope; stoic, bearded, and – in the inversion of the photograph – deathly, horrifically pale.

I stepped away from the picture, feeling my stomach beginning to twitch with nausea. I felt a terrible temptation to peer into the hundred-gallon tub and look at the old captain's face. I imagined his ghostly appearance – as bleached and bleary as the photograph – his grey beard turning white, the tips translucent, his once windburnt skin resolving to paper. I needed to get out of the hold. I left the worthless photographs where they lay and staggered back towards the door, kicking the tarp from its frame. I did not fancy returning to that faded parliament of specimens to turn off the electric lantern – and by its faint glow I swear I could dimly perceive, reflected in the glass screen of the tub, the ghostly colour negative of a long drowned man.

At mess I asked Dr. Whelan if he could take my half of the watch that night, as I was feeling nauseous. He thought for a while and assented, if I would take his half tomorrow. Just as well. I went to bed early and slept fitfully, rocked to bed by the serrations of the swell, thinking about sleep as the darkroom where the daily impress of the retina is developed, and praying that the negatives would not be nightmarish – pallid – underexposed.

***

The next day Dr. Whelan called for us to lay the trawl again. The sky was the same oppressive pall of white it had been since the storm began, the sea was grey and limpid, and there was no sign of life or land in sight. Food and fuel were still in good supply, but the mood was fidgety, agitated. No one could quite believe that we hadn't been seen by another ship yet – or indeed, seen another ship ourselves. But Dr. Whelan tried to maintain morale by keeping us at our task. The trawl was shaken out and winched overboard just as we had done before, I stretched my aching back in preparation for another capstan carousel. We watched the winch whir as it unreeled the tow warp. Red bands flickered past us with alarming speed. Eight hundred feet, nine hundred feet, one thousand feet. We stared on in disbelief as the fifteenth red mark whizzed by, then the sixteenth, then the seventeenth. Two thousand feet. Two thousand one hundred. Two thousand two hundred. And then the winch creaked into inactivity. The trawl lurked below us at a depth of two hundred and seventy-five fathoms.

'We must be over the deepest part of the North Sea', murmured Whelan, 'but that's not possible. Sermon – how far did we trawl yesterday?'. Sermon held up eight fingers. 'Nautical miles is it?'. He nodded. 'We were trawling for an hour and a half, speed – four or five knots. I don't think the depth changes so abruptly here'. The captain's charts confirmed it. The deckhand butted in. 'We would have seen the winch rolling if we were trawling downhill, doc. And what's more', he paused, puzzled, 'we've been at anchor since we raised the trawl. We can't have drifted in the night'. The crew all turned to see the anchor-chain descending into the stony surf. 'Maybe it's come loose in some current?' I proffered. 'Maybe', said the doctor, sceptically, 'though I think we would have felt it'. Soon the anchor was raised – and it *was* raised. The steel grapnel was still attached and in perfect order. 'This chain's not even a thousand feet, doc. It was just hanging off down there. Current could have done it, maybe'. Dr. Whelan's brows were knitted with doubt. 'But what current? And we can't have miscalculated the depth so badly. As you say, the bottom trawl would have told us'. Soon Sermon had slunk off to the wheelhouse, and it was quietly agreed that we would, for the time being, abandon the ratiocination of these rather disconcerting anomalies, and run the trawl.

It was a gloomy and perplexing hour. Dr. Whelan was deep in thought, looking distantly out over the flat grey sea. I did the same. It struck me that I hadn't seen a single seabird since the storm, nor even so much as a white feather bobbing on the waves. I couldn't blame them for shyness, I thought, under this straitjacket of a sky.

The trawl came up slowly, slower than before. We were all more tired than before. And more apprehensive. Each rotation of the winch was like the cranking of a hideous jack-in-the-box. My guts tightened with every turn of the capstan, like tension in some hidden spring. When the trawl emerged, I thought, something would release – something terrifying. Around and around we went, little red flags slowly wrapping wetly around the winch like the tendrils of some sanguine vine. And then the trawl began to loom. A dark metallic shape beneath the surface of the water, growing larger and larger, preparing to breach. I imagined I could hear its chains clinking below, amplified by the density of the dark, freezing fluid, driving deep into my eardrums. And then it emerged. Sermon manned the crane again – and I loaded my camera like a gun.

It wasn't long before Dr. Whelan's exclamation. 'What on earth?' he began, and speech seemed to fail him. 'What on earth?'

The identification trays were positively heaving with what seemed at first like squid. Speckled bullets of gently pulsating flesh, crowned with a tangle of tentacles, jewelled with cold and queerly intelligent eyes. Most were unusually slender creatures. 'Some deep-sea variety, doc?'. Other small life crawled erratically amid the oozing pile and sediment fine as moondust, but Dr. Whelan's attention was entirely on the cephalopods. He had taken off his leather glove, designed to protect against urchins and stinging worms, and was mechanically picking up and squeezing each and every squid in the pile, replacing them dumbly. 'This can't be true', he said, again and again, 'this just can't be!'. 'What is it?' I asked him, 'what's wrong with them?' 'Wrong with them? Wrong with them? Here, Albert, feel this – no, feel it! Do you feel it?' To my utter disgust the scientist was pressing a small squid into my hand, guiding my thumb along its mantle. Were it not for the lanyard I would have dropped my camera. I drew away in loathing and wiped my slimy hand on my coat, throwing the squid back into the tray. It felt cold as the abyss. 'No,' I managed, stammering slightly as the doctor looked at me askance, 'No, I don't feel it. I don't feel it. What is it?'. The doctor took a deep breath.

'They're belemnites', he said, 'living belemnites. You can feel the bone in their back'.

I took his word for it. The creatures looked just like squids to me – but squids always were uncanny creatures, I thought, precariously balanced on the verge of the alien. 'These creatures', said Whelan slowly, 'died out at the end of the Cretaceous period. And these ones look even more primitive than that. Gentlemen, this is not normal. This is *not normal.* Look how many there are! I just – I refuse to believe that a lingering population of *belemnites* could have survived in the *North Sea*, of all places, with all the fishing and trawling and travel and trade… no. No! This simply cannot be. And yet…'

He picked up another, and delicately traced the mineralised ridge of the phragmocone, that primitive structure which men have observed in veins of raw green marble, and never before in quivering flesh. 'It is. It has to be! We are', the doctor smiled, 'in uncharted waters, now'.

I filled a reel of film with belemnites, and in spite of my feeble protestations about the lighting, Dr. Whelan asked me to fill another. I watched Groff go up and down to the hold, fetching more jars, fetching more preservative. Eventually the deckhand cleared his throat. 'Doc, there's a problem'. 'A problem?' 'Yes. We're running low on formaldehyde'. 'What?' 'We're running low on formaldehyde'. 'What about the alcohol from the first expedition?' 'We used that up before the storm'. Dr. Whelan put down his specimens and stared coldly at the deckhand. 'Where did it go?' 'Sorry?' 'The formaldehyde. We brought enough for six weeks at least'. 'Well', said the younger man slowly, 'I can tell you where eighty-odd gallons went'.

There was a silence. Dr. Whelan was biting the inside of his mouth. 'Tap some off' he said.

'Sorry?' 'I said draw some of it off! I can't throw away any of these specimens, Groff. These are the first belemnites anyone has seen, ever. Scientists, museums worldwide will be frothing at the chops for a sample to study. I can't just chuck them overboard like bycatch! Now go. Draw off ten gallons from the captain's tub, there's a valve at the bottom. Twenty gallons maybe. That'll leave him enough, yes? Do you hear me! Go!' 'I don't think-' 'just GO!'

And the younger man disappeared belowdecks. Leaning overboard, I quietly threw up.

\*\*\*

Second watch that night was meant to be Dr. Whelan's, but owing to our agreement, the duty had fallen to me. I had spent the evening clearing out the sorting tray of stragglers and silt with the deckhand, who was unusually sullen, and looked like he had seen a ghost. His was the first watch, and I was exhausted, but I thought I would wake up half an hour before the changeover to see if the day's photographs had turned out any better. Part of me did not want to set foot in the hold again. But part of me knew that the camera was all I had. If I didn't develop these photographs, I thought, my mind would regress – would turn to dark places, or rather, pale things. I had to keep the dead at bay.

I relaxed myself with the old familiar process, paying no attention to the rows and rows of newly filled jars, the unearthly pallor of the belemnites whose pigment had already been leeched to the point of near-albinism. The fish we had caught on the first trawl after the storm had turned almost completely white, the weird mechanisms of its jaw and gills distended in an expression of anoxic pain. The specimens had grown so pale as to appear luminous, though I knew this to be an artefact of my own adjusting vision, a mere trick of the darkness. Into the shadowy well of the development tank went the two reels of the day. I prepared the developer, using the five minutes' preparation to regulate my breathing. Next the bleach fixer, similarly prepared, and finally – I reached for the stabiliser. My fingers knocked the bottle. It was empty. I began to breathe faster, cursing under my breath. I can't lose these photographs. I can't let the living colour of these ancient things be forgotten; I cannot let extinction claim them for a second time. These pictures are my arrows against death! I began to panic. I had forgotten to look for my extra supplies, and there was no time to leave the hold now: the pictures were developing that very instant. I had a minute at most before they were ruined. I had to think – and quickly. Water wouldn't do it, and I couldn't just take them out – when it struck me, strangled me, forced out a terrible groan. What else had the early lithograph photographers used to stabilise their pictures – but *paraformaldehyde?*

I maintain that I had no choice. The photographs had become talismanic, and in that moment, there was nothing more important than their preservation. I leapt to the sample-racks, switching on the electric lantern. The thought crossed my mind, that I might potentially extract some stabilising agent from one of the jars – but they were tightly sealed, and there was no clean way to get the stuff out. I did what I must when I reached for Captain Swope's tub. There's a valve at the bottom… somewhere – here! The damage had been done, I thought, the precedent had been set – I only needed a few drops to dilute. I knocked the valve and nothing came out. I winced. 'I'm so sorry, captain'. I turned the valve slightly, catching a few drops of formaldehyde in the funnel, which I topped up rapidly with warm water and agitated. Paraformaldehyde became formaldehyde when dissolved in warm water, I remembered, then it could fix tissues – perhaps then it could fix photographic pigments? It had only been a few drops. A few drops wouldn't hurt him. In my panicked state, I hazarded a glance at the preservation tub. It was a glance which filled me with instant regret. The levels of preservative had declined as if in drought, and the captain, wound in his white rags of thermal linen, had sunk deeper to accommodate it. His limbs were cocked in horrible rubbery bends like those of an unborn child, his hair and beard were white as seafoam, and his *face*… It was as if I had taken a photograph without a camera, and the image of that gurning axolotl, that ghastly puffed cave-thing, would develop in my brain forever and ever. I thanked god I had been sick earlier as I cracked open the development tank and rinsed the photographs. It had only been a drop, I thought, only a drop.

A cry sounded from above. It sounded again, louder than before. Groff was calling me to my watch? Perhaps I was late. I would have to review the wretched photographs later, I thought, hoping that my desperate efforts had not been in vain – and then the call came a third time. 'Ship! Ship ho!' I bundled out onto the deck. Groff was gesticulating madly, bellowing to catch the crew's attention. Dr. Whelan was already there, wearing the captain's old nautical jumper. 'Look, look! Can you see it – there! That shape! Ship ho! Where's the flare gun?', cried the deckhand, 'somebody get me the flare gun!' 'Where's the flare gun?' asked the doctor, 'I don't know!'. 'It's moving fast! Get the bloody flare gun!' 'I don't know where it is!' 'Come on! Ship! Ship ho! Help! Help!' There was a definite shape out there in the night ocean, silent and indistinct, but as powerfully present as gravity or infrasound. But it was passing. I joined the doctor and the deckhand in shouting, trying frantically to get its attention. And then it had passed. We could all sense it go, diminishing from earshot, its bow-waves brushing our hull. 'Why didn't you have the flare gun?' raged the doctor. Groff assumed a dangerously pugilistic stance. 'You didn't bloody give it to me when you took Kenspeckle's watch'. 'That's because I didn't have it, you idiot. I thought Sermon had it. But he didn't give it to me after his shift or else I'd bloody have it, wouldn't I!?' Groff spat. 'Don't speak to me like that, *mate*'.

'Where's Sermon?' I asked. The two men stepped away from each other. The engineer had not, it appeared been roused by the shouting. We checked his bunk and the engine room. Not there. We finally found him, strangely enough, on deck. He was standing astern in his oilskins, holding a fishing-pole, and looking out at the sea. 'Sermon', asked Dr. Whelan breathlessly, 'have you been up here all night? Where's the bloody flare gun? You had it last'.

The engineer reeled in his line and cast again. A soft splash. He looked at the doctor and shrugged his shoulders, shaking his head. He put the butt of the angling pole under his armpit.

*No fish*, he signed, *no fish*.

∗∗∗

'Today we trawl again'.

There had never been a drearier day on the *Ronnoch Mor*. The white sky had never seemed so close. A depressive weight was sagging everybody's shoulders like a wet towel. The sea was slate-grey, sluggish and forbidding. Nobody had slept. And everyone was angry at everyone else.

It would have been easy enough, I remember thinking, to mutiny. Dr. Whelan couldn't *force* us to lay the trawl again. We could simply refuse – and I had half a mind to. But routine, I knew, was important. Maybe hard work would heal the wounds of the previous night. And besides – if I wasn't up here dredging, I'd be down in the hold working on my photographs. The events of the night had not pressed my guilt out of mind. It was only a few drops, I told myself. No spirit ever stalked for so meagre a desecration. But they *were* a few drops, and in those few drops, no doubt, were a few particles of the captain's colour. They were my albatross. And I could not close my eyes for long before the negatives appeared.

We watched the trawl descend with weary expectation. The winch gave a banshee buzz. Already it had dropped to two thousand feet. Two thousand one hundred. Two hundred. We prepared for it to settle. Three hundred. Four hundred. Five hundred. Our eyes grew wide. At this length the tow-warps were still bright and shiny. They had never been immersed. Two thousand six hundred. Seven. Eight. Nine. The winch gave a clunk. We were out of cable.

And then the *Ronnoch Mor* began to tilt ever so slightly towards her stern. 'We're three thousand feet deep', said the deckhand slowly, 'and we still haven't touched the bottom. How deep is the North Sea supposed to be, doc?' Dr. Whelan didn't answer. 'Not that deep', I said.

We didn't trawl for long. Only the doctor seemed to have any heart for the job, and even his enthusiasm now seemed somehow perverse. We ground the sockets of our knees in turning the great wheel, watching the little red flags wind up again. I was almost too weary to dread what might emerge. The great trawl became more and more visible, it was the shadow of the *Ronnoch Mor*, growing longer and darker in some ashy, final sunset. None of us had seen a sunset in weeks. Nor even a sunrise. Only a flat sky whose pallor did not bear contemplation.

I did not want to be present when the trawl was spilled out. I went instead to get my camera – and paused when I heard the mast-crane release. I knew something exciting had happened before I even heard the doctor's laughter. Emerging onto the deck, I was immediately struck by a tremendous, briny stench – the tang of ammonium, of natal salinity. The doctor was grinning like a man possessed, while the solemn deckhand simply stood transfixed. There was not a speck of mud on the sorting tray, hardly a single droplet of detritus – and I thought for a minute that the trawl had simply failed, that we hadn't gone for long enough, that we hadn't even reached the bottom. And then I moved closer. The mineral reek of the sea was overwhelming. There, on the sorting tray, almost indistinguishable from the pooling seawater, was a varicose lump of translucent jelly. Globs of mucus were sloughing from its flanks, becoming invisible where they slipped beneath the surface, save for the shadow of faint veins. And not simply sloughing, I realised, they were *moving* – a hundred glassy smears of matter, pulsating, reforming, looping and twisting; probing with pseudopods, dividing and conglobing into still more and still greater masses of protean *stuff*. Dr. Whelan passed the slime through his ungloved fingers, shuddering. He picked something up from the bottom of the tray, a drop of detritus, I thought – and held it to the dumb, directionless sky. The legs of a tiny bronze trilobite moved in concertina waveforms; migrating shadows across a field of white. He gave the trilobite an appalling kiss.

'Groff', he called, 'fetch the preservative. Everything we have. Yes, drain it from the captain, damn his rotten bones. Siphon it all. Go now. Now. NOW. And Albert' – he turned to me, extending a hand – 'your services would be greatly appreciated'.

An age seemed to pass. 'No', I said finally, my voice quavering. 'I can't, Dr. Whelan. I can't. These things – these *things* – are not meant to be preserved. This time should have passed aeons ago. Sometimes, it is only right, that death… has its way'. He stared at me as if I had been spouting nonsense, and I became acutely conscious that on some level, I had been. My face reddened. '*Death*, Albert Kenspeckle? Give me that'. He snatched the camera from around my neck, breaking the lanyard at one end. I gasped. He turned it around in his hands, levelled its glassy eye at me, then at the collecting trays with their slimy treasure. 'Not death, Kenspeckle. In fact, I believe I have found my immortality. Now', the scientist spat, 'go and help the deckhand'.

I went down to my bunk and wrapped myself in blankets, intending to stay there until the *Ronnoch Mor* was rescued or ran out of supplies. Until death knocked to claim me, I thought.

I wasn't waiting long.

'Albert'.

A voice was coming from the door. I pressed my face against the cotsides, and was reminded of weathering the storm, that ghastly, bleak, unnatural storm that had stranded the *Ronnoch Mor* in space and time, the storm that killed her captain –

'Albert'.

I turned. Otis Groff, the deckhand, was standing there. He held a can in one hand and reeked of formaldehyde. I turned away. How could he do that to poor Captain Swope, I thought, how could he live with himself – *only a few drops*. I gagged. I turned to face him.

'I know where the flare gun is'.

'What?'

'The flare gun. Whelan's been hiding it, god knows why. It's up in the cap's cabin where he sleeps now. In the floor hatch, with the whiskey'.

'How do you-' I began. 'Door was ajar. Remembered there were supplies in the hatches – and I didn't want to mess with the old man a second time, you know'. *Only a few drops*. 'Except I had to. Look, I don't have much time, gotta help doc clear up. Cap's quarters. Floor hatch'.

And he left. And I soon followed him. Down to the room which had once belonged to old Captain Swope, where the door was still ajar. I crept in. The old captain's nautical austerity had been overrun by Whelan's rather less refined aesthetic preferences, which largely consisted of improbable scientific instruments and biological *memento mori*. The bookshelf (with a locked front for high weather) was stashed with oceanographical opuscula; logs from the *Challenger* expedition, treatises on invertebrate paleobiology, and outdated *Coast Pilots*. All worthless, I thought, as my eye zeroed in on the floor hatch. It came up without trouble – revealing the flare gun's brick-red emergency case, and a few unaccounted-for bottles of whiskey and rum. Just as Groff had said. I opened the flare gun case and took out the weapon. My heart was racing. It would be less suspicious to smuggle it out alone, I thought, carefully following the instructions on the case's lid to load a flare, and slipping the other two in my pocket. I heard footsteps above, and the rungs of the short ladder creaking. I cursed under my breath. Dr. Whelan was coming down. If he should catch me here… I stopped breathing entirely, falling completely silent. I heard seawater dripping from the trawl-apparatus. Drip, drip, drip. *Only a few drops.* A man moved along the corridor. He came closer and closer – and further, and further. I breathed a sigh of relief. He wasn't coming back to his quarters. But where was he going? Another hollow clanging as a ladder was descended. My eyes narrowed. The hold! He was going to the hold – and all my photographs were there!

I shouldered open the cabin door and slowly crept out. The sea would conceal any accidental noises, but something as regular as footsteps had to be suppressed. I moved slowly, painfully slowly; descending the same few stairs with unbelievable trepidation, the loaded flare gun, gaudy in its chipped red paint, trembling in my knuckly hand. I thought of all the hideous pale things floating behind that door. I thought of the slumped cadaver of Captain

Swope, wrinkled with moisture, exposed to the elements, dribbling the yellowish plasma of preservation, pale as my own ghastly negatives. And then I thought of the despicable Dr. Whelan – and kicked open the hold. A raggedy bolt of tarpaulin skidded across the floor. He was there. I saw him horrifically aglow in the wan light of the electric lantern, eyes wide and white; my own camera dangling from his neck by its repaired lanyard. In his hands was my photographic development tank. He leered at me terribly, drawing back his lips in a ghastly smile of knowing. 'Now, Mr. Kenspeckle – where do you keep your stabilising agent?'

In that moment, in the faint but clinical radiance of the electric lantern, I saw the doctor for what he truly was. He was as lifelessly pale as the old man, who I could vaguely perceive curled up through the windowed sides of his barren tank. He was as impossibly leeched of all life as those rows upon rows of raw and flabby flesh which caught the anaemic light and pulsed with pasty malevolence. They were all ghosts. The captain, the specimens, the doctor – everything was, in the cosmic circus of evolution, a ghost, a ghost of what came before. Behind the white mask of Dr. Whelan's grimace was a grimacing ape, long dead, behind it a lizard, behind it a fish, behind it a belemnite, all dead yet all present, present in his every feature, present down to the most primitive urschleim that ever spawned life in the eldritch gulfs below! We were nature's negatives, I saw, and we were constantly developing. But I could not let those photographs develop. That dark tank was Pandora's pyxis. Within it were all the ghosts that haunt this earth. They must not be released.

I wheeled at the doctor with my flare gun. He dropped the box and leapt for cover, the upper lid clattering. This unnatural evolution ends here. The flare leapt from the barrel and exploded against the tank, filling the hold with a dazzling magnesium glow. Beyond the ringing in my ears I could hear Dr. Whelan screaming. I nocked another flare, and aiming at the specimen jars, let loose another torrent of destruction. The formaldehyde erupted into liquid flame, dousing the hold, completely consuming – I noticed with glee through the dizzying tracers and afterglow – the photographs I had already developed. Good. I put the final flare in the gun and nuzzled the round barrel under my jaw. I saw how the formaldehyde was drooling into the tub, how the old captain's sodden thermals were sprouting beautiful trailing tongues of blue-green-orange fire. I smiled and closed my eyes. It looked like a photograph in perfect colour.

# TOADSTONE AND WITCH HAZEL

I withdrew my hand and regretted it immediately. How ill-behaved I must have appeared! His touch held the old shiver of routine inspection, and there was something perverse about the way his thumb had brushed the ring, like a greengrocer dusting a fat button mushroom. 'I'm sorry', I started, expecting raised eyebrows but receiving only a kindly smile, 'I would take it off to show you more closely but my fingers are sore and a bit swollen. It fits tighter than I thought'. 'No apologies needed', he said nicely, 'and certainly no need to take it off. I can tell you what I think it is – bufonite. Bufonite of a quite unusual variety'. He scratched his head at my bafflement, disarraying a faded rose-gold combover. 'Sometimes called "toadstone"'.

'Mama used to call it that, I think'. A figment returned to my memory. 'She told me she cut the jewel from the head of a big brown puddock, who was a devil'. His smile was the same handsome, apologetic smile he gave the parents at his clinic after inoculation tantrums, the same gentle smile I always received after a chiding for my poor circulation. It was familiar but never comfortable, because he was an apothecary, and could not be trusted. I am glad Dr. Brundich hadn't felt – or at least hadn't mentioned – the coldness of my hands. 'Elizana', he began, 'I know things are still sensitive and it's a good thing to hold on to your mother's memory –' he looked at the toadstone ring '– and no-one could blame you for that, especially moving back here. But much of what Mother Tatwine used to tell you...' he slowed to choose his words carefully '...wasn't all *right*. Toadstones don't come from toads. They are the teeth of a fish which lived and died a very long time ago and have turned to stone. Nothing more'.

I wanted to ask how a tooth could turn into a stone, which sounded preposterous. But I didn't want to argue with my old family doctor, in the hallway of the house I had been born in, a short week after Mama's death. I didn't want to argue with anyone. I wanted to be by myself.

'Is it valuable?' 'Maybe. It looks like a fairly large one, although – if you hold it up to your ear and give it a shake, yes, just like that – it seems to have come a little loose in its fitting, which is only natural with old things like this. The ring itself is antique, by my reckoning. Lords and ladies used to wear these sorts of rings because they thought the bufonite could detect poison, you know. It was meant to change colour or something'. Yes, this much I knew – for now I really could remember Mama's lesson. The puddock is a deadly venomous creature, and the toadstone in its head kept it safe from itself. 'But I hope you don't mean to sell it, Elizana', the doctor continued, 'I know Mother Tatwine really wanted you to have it. Even more than the house. It was very valuable to *her-*' 'yes, thank you, doctor. It's valuable to me. Thank you… for your help. And about the ring', I said, feeling myself cower with embarrassment. 'Don't mention it. Keep well, Elizana, and please call me if you need help settling in. The keys are on the hall table'. He turned, preparing to leave. 'My condolences again. And Elizana-' I froze, terrified '-it is good to see you after all these years'. 'You as well, doctor. Thank you. Bye'. 'Goodbye now'.

And then I was alone in the hallway I could remember half from childhood, half from dream. I walked into the sitting room, feeling the boards creak. Everything was sheeted in a blue glamour of dust. China in the cabinets, doilies on the tea-table like cobwebby dreamcatchers. Withered grey herbs in greenware pots on the windowsill. Her wicker-backed rocking chair which I had picked away at nervously as a girl. On the mantlepiece, porcelain bric-a-brac, and above, our portrait. She with her loose blue dress, shawl, and disfigurement – me a pale child of seven or eight with watery eyes and a hand which closed around two of her fingers. It was an awful picture, I thought, putting a hand to my face, finding relief in the cool. I had never liked the portrait – I had cried while we posed for it – and I had suffered the switch afterwards. Mama had been indomitable. She would be angry, I thought, if I took the picture down, just as she was always angry when I picked at the wicker furniture she had woven when my nerves took over. I was guilty and glad there had been no funeral. Mama had detested sacrament, as Dr. Brundich reminded me, when I grew anxious about 'what her friends would think'. 'Unfortunately, Elizana, I don't believe that is a pressing concern'. Even Dr. Brundich had no idea precisely what had happened to Mama when she died, and he had been one of the few people left who had known her. The medical records had been improperly completed – and as far as we knew, my mother didn't even have a grave. I twisted her toadstone ring on my finger. I wondered – if there had been an open casket affair – would the morticians have tried to cover up that face of hers? The portraitist had shown no such decorum. I could scarcely bear to hold her gaze in the picture. Indeed, I could scarcely bear to hold my own.

Most of my belongings had already been delivered to the new address, except for the television, for which I presently made some space in the sitting room. Upstairs I hesitated before the master bedchamber, eventually opening the door to the spare – my old room. I'd settle here. To sleep in her room would be unthinkable. The walls were bare and speckled faintly with small fingerprints only visible when the light came in through the window at a slant. Somehow, I thought, I would need to get the nursery bars removed. I dusted the wicker lampshade and the empty bookshelf and straightened the blue rug I had crumpled while making the bed with my new white sheets. The rug was thinner in the middle, like the skin of an aged tambourine. I stocked the wardrobe with the knot in its grain that had looked distressingly like an eye when I was little. I was faintly excited to begin making this space my own. The school where I worked three days a week as a teaching assistant would not be open for a while – I could bring in a desk, hang some pictures, maybe even get a fishbowl and some goldfish before the holidays were over. In fact, I could do all sorts of other things that had once been strictly forbidden, both by Mama and by the miserable landlord of my now-former apartment. But this would do for now. I washed in the bathroom across and laid down on the bed, which felt smaller. The room felt somehow *closer* than I remembered; the oaken hull of the wardrobe was somehow more intrusive, the lampshade lower, the walls pressing further in. The door had never closed properly. But it would do for now.

That bed had borne the impression of too many fitful nights. I awoke unrested, having slept very poorly, with a sensation in my cheeks and forehead like wet rawhide shrinking. I didn't need the bathroom mirror to tell me that the insidious pink leaven was rising again. I put my cold hands to my face to soothe it and quickly put them down again. This always happened. When I was anxious – when I was home. She was always angry when I picked at the wicker. My hands went up to my face, to a particularly sore spot to the side of my nose. I kept my fingernails short because I knew what damage I could do, but that was no impediment. I picked away at the spot, watching it puff up like a nettle sting, gently desperate to relieve the dull tension which throbbed harder with every thought – but no. No no. I splashed my face with cold water to try and counteract the swelling I had inflicted; it pulsed ugly pink like a bubble in rhubarb jam. I felt my head beginning to ache. Not again. Water splashed. I held back my twitching fingers. I had gone so long without this anguish that I almost thought I had escaped it – but perhaps I never really had. Perhaps it had always been there, dormant as a spore, brewing just beneath my skin.

Mama had a lesson about this. I left the bathroom with my back towards the mirror, descending straight into the kitchen. At least I had nowhere to be but here, I thought, as I opened the shallow drawers beneath the counter, rooting through a rat's nest of old phone numbers and finely labelled paper bags filled with seeds: hellebore, goatsbeard, mountain germander. And there was Mama's recipe book, just as I remembered, bound in fraying olive cloth, lolling with a hundred tongues of yellowed paper. I had received many lessons from this book as a girl, and not just cookery. Lessons about gardening, medicine, even some funny little rhymes whose cadences, impressed in the waxy cell of my brain, even now lent shape to my memory. Her sidelong handwriting accused me faintly as I leafed through its pages, as if the book knew unsupervised consultations were forbidden – so that even when I found the note that I sought, I received, in place of satisfaction, only a dubious pang of guilt. *For Tenderness of the Skin*', it read, '*Apply Tea Brewed from the Leaves of Witch Hazel'*. A small sketch of the plant in question followed, beside the greygreen parchment of a pressed leaf. My face throbbed and I could not resist the urge to calm its seething surface with cool fingertips. Now even small movements of my mouth and eyebrows triggered ripples of pain. I returned Mama's recipe book to the drawer in exactly the same position I had found it, meticulously rearranging its nest of seed-bags and paper-scraps like humble offerings on a peasant grave. No-one would know it had been disturbed, I thought, as I hastened to the garden for my remedy.

The garden had grown unruly in Mama's absence. Not that it had ever been a particularly agreeable place, with its curious banks of herbs, arranged by their virtues, and unusually stunted graft-trees lurching in the long grass by the biscuity drystone wall. Rotting leaves like bruises formed a colourful scum on the surface of the large pond sunk in their shadow, its boggy margins dense with marsh simples and the beached pontoons of water lilies. I picked my way towards the bottom of the garden, feeling the ground sag and the grass clog with moisture. The brown water smelled like rain worms and old fruit. There was the witch hazel shrub, low and sprawling, its sprays lightly honeyed with the last of summer. My footsteps echoed through my skin. Fifteen years ago, on the afternoon of the day we had posed for our portrait, I had watched Mama approach this tree between greenware pots of dried herbs on the windowsill; watched her clip a fistful of branches, and felt them strike me, again and again.

I stopped picking at my face and broke off a spray, feeling the wood crack through me. My aching head nearly bowed me over. Turning away I noticed ripples in the pond. Just beneath the leafy surface was a large fish – a carp of some kind, perhaps, with knurled and muddy scales. Its broad mouth champed convulsively at the air, breaking the water, giving off the uncomfortable impression of laughter.

✳✳✳

I set a pot to boil on the stove, stripping the spray of witch hazel and tying the twigs and leaves together with twine to steep, just the way Mama had done. Sometimes, I remembered, Mama had withheld her lessons and her treatments when I had been naughty. The water bubbled through me. It suddenly struck me that, in the two days I had been living in this house I had inherited, not one moment of them had been truly spent alone. I poured the tea into a bowl, fetched a cloth, and waited so that the temperature would not further irritate my skin. Another figment returned to my memory – was not this house built out of figments and memories? Imitating her motions with an exactness only instinct can assure, I dipped the toadstone ring into the tea. Mama had done this with every salve and spirit she distilled towards the end of her life, I recalled, as if old age had made her paranoid of the poisons in her own pantry. There was no change in the ring. The tea would be safe. Good. I took the bowl into the sitting room, sat in her rocking chair; one hand unweaving its armrest and the other picking at the cloth. The artist had not merely been indecorous, I thought, but *cruel* – to render a little girl of seven or eight with tears in her eyes and every blemish budding beneath the red fringe on her forehead. I couldn't bear to do it in her presence, creaking my way instead to the bathroom mirror. I mopped my face with witch hazel tea. It smelled bitter. It had a medicinal sting which was comforting, although by the time I had wrung the last drop from my cloth my brow felt more rufous and volcanic than before. My fingers twitched to probe its topography; whether or not I succumbed I cannot remember. I went to bed while the light still slanted through the nursery bars, picking out fingerprints like ghostly pores on the bare and shivering wall.

I woke soon after dawn the next morning with a face like a pincushion. The pressure of my cheek against the pillow was unbearable. Cold water could not quench it; the bathroom mirror reflected a horrendously swollen serpigo of spots like strawberry seeds. A dull pain needled down from every follicle – this tension could not go unrelieved. My fingers worked spasmodically, automatically, excavating tiny beads of tallow, leaving craters which filled like goblets of blood. My skin was a network of dungeons, each speck of sebum was a demon helot, and my fingers pressed and pinched and dug and picked with the force of an exorcism. Sometimes the waxy yellow substance would wriggle out like a maggot. Other times it would pop out like the amber bulb of a young daffodil. Soon my face was pale and puffed with lymph, numb enough to grimace with: it was like weeding, I thought with some hysteria, my skin was like a sensitive soil in which unmentionable sprouts had festered into incubation by the light of a lunatic moon. Both my cheeks and forehead had been utterly excoriated by the time I realised how entirely I had lost control. Disgusted, I anointed myself with cold water, hoping to shrink those ghastly protuberances whose bulging had utterly distorted my lineaments – to absolutely no effect. I knew I needed another dose of Mama's witch hazel tea – and stumbled downstairs. Mercifully I had not spilled out the rest of the pot – and transferring its contents once more into a bowl, I bore it painfully back up to the bathroom. The toadstone rattled more than usual as I immersed it in the witch hazel brew – revealing no change. Thank the sun and stars. I splashed myself with the cold infusion, feeling my flesh throb like drumskin. My heart pounded like a mad drummer. The familiar antiseptic burn. The invigorating balm of the cold.

Though I could see myself reddening where it worked into my flesh, the tea was soothing me back into myself, from frenzy back to guilt, from hatred into worry. I could never understand this desire to unravel the wicker, to unpick the fibres of my being. As a girl I had not thought upon it, indeed, by the time I left home, I had no reason to think upon it: by then my condition had almost fully receded. But now it had returned with me. Mama was dead, I thought, and with her all the wretchedness of my childhood. But I could not shake the feeling that she too, somehow, had returned – or worse still, had never truly left me; had remained sequestered somewhere deep within, and had only now seized her chance to ooze back into being through the weeping portals of my flesh. Even now I felt my eyes focusing on the few unruptured pustules on my temples and my hairline, my fingers twitching to exhume her, to unwrap the membranous winding sheet of my own skin and reveal her in the mirror. All would be lost, I thought, if those fingers stayed idle. I would be lost. And while I waited for my face to dry, I occupied them in scrubbing all the ghostly little fingerprints from my childhood walls. Then I took down the wicker lampshade and unravelled it entirely.

Though the swelling had indeed begun to subside, my face ached torturously and I was smitten by the terrible panic that – like the pale convolutions at the bottom of a dandelion root, or the stumps of the Lernean serpent – I had not completely excavated my deepest cavities of their redoubted Insider, the Insider regrowing with doubled ferocity. My cold, blessedly cold fingers scouted its hard bumps, the Insider's fortifications – and found that it was ever so easy for a touch to become a press, to become a pinch, become a squeeze. I could feel myself slipping into a vicious continuum. There was only so much wickerwork in the house to unpick, and that, I knew, would only enrage her. I would spiralise myself like a pencil carefully sharpened. I would destroy every handhold by which I might crawl out of the abyss. I would go into the garden and pick more of the witch hazel, brew more of the tea. And, though the prospect made me faint with nerves, I knew I would have to talk to Dr. Brundich.

The breeze hurt where I felt it on my face. The garden hissed and shivered pale with tumbled undersides of leaves; the afternoon was so overcast that I suddenly understood how the carp in the pond must feel with scum blotting out its sky. I could just about discern the great fish sluggishly circling beneath the dark surface, see the dull flash of its tarnished bronze chainmail, the flicker of its bony fins, as I tiptoed towards the low and skulking shrub; pruning knife poised between my fingers, hilt clinking nervously against my toadstone ring. *Her* toadstone ring. *Her* witch hazel. Soon I had stripped every extraneous twig I could reach; every lingering flower and leafy offshoot, and was bearing the bushel back to the kitchen: encumbered as that sorry harvestman whose bent shadow falls nightly on the pocked and craterous countenance of the moon.

Steam from the cookpot brought warmth to my bones, and with it returned the dull incessant pain, a pain which had steadily grown in intensity each time I let my traitorous fingers wander. I would use as much of the witch hazel as would fit in the vessel, would brew it for as long as I could bear to wait. The remedy had been effective, but it had been insufficient. This time I could not take any chances. Would Mama be proud of me, I thought, for finally putting her lessons to proper use? I hoped that she was. The sorest spots on my face were beginning to harden into great cystic lumps, bacterial magma chambers bubbling far beneath mounds of solid flesh. My physiognomy was in a state of almost geological upheaval. I felt like my face had grown new features, new organs of sense which detected only pain. I couldn't go outside in this state, I realised

– the short walk to the clinic would be unbearable, and of course I couldn't let anyone see me – especially not the apothecary. How he would scold me if he knew! I took the infusion off the boil and put it by the window, slumping down into the rocking chair. I held my breath and dialled Dr. Brundich. Splinters threaded the rug beneath me. Idle fingers crawled about the toadstone ring, rotating the jewel in its dull gold fitting.

'Hello?' 'Hello – doctor I think I need your help'. 'Hello Elizana'. 'Hello-' 'Did the television arrive this morning?' 'No it didn't'. 'Okay'. *Science is as wicked as sacrament, Elizana.* 'I'm sorry?' 'I didn't say anything-' 'Hello?' 'Yes, doctor, I'm sorry, hello. I think – yes, I think I need your help'. 'What seems to be the problem?' 'My – my skin. Something's happened to my skin and I don't know what – am I going to die?' 'I'm sorry?' 'My skin. Something's wrong with my skin. Very wrong.' 'Can you describe the symptoms?' A pause. I had no idea what he meant. 'Doctor, what's happening to me?' 'Elizana, please don't panic. Listen, I'm just coming back into town – I can stop by for a visit-' 'No! Sorry-' 'Elizana if this is serious I can put you in touch with a dermatologist in-' 'No, no, no, no, no – I just want to know what's happening-' 'I can't-' 'Please?' The receiver boiled against my cheek.

'Look'. The doctor's voice was pained and ponderous. 'Elizana – do you remember Mother Tatwine's – condition?' 'Her disfigurement?' 'Her condition. She would never let me treat it, nor offer so much as an official diagnosis. But you see sometimes – when a mother or a father has a condition – they can pass it onto their children. Sometimes they can even pass on the likelihood of a condition, even if the condition isn't really that serious. Or even a feature. Just like you have Mother Tatwine's cold hands. And my – and my red hair'. 'Mama laid a curse on me then' I said, 'but why? Why would she do such a thing when I loved her? Didn't she know how much I loved her?' The exasperation in the doctor's voice filled me with still greater anxiety. I began to pick at my forehead, staining my fingertips pink. 'No, no, Elizana, listen, she did nothing of the sort – look, listen, please. It's just another thing you've inherited from her – like the house, like the bufonite ring.' 'I don't-' 'Look, if it makes it easier to understand, sure, yes it's a bit like a curse – a genetic curse. You have a bit of Mother Tatwine inside you Elizana – the bit that sometimes gives you painful skin. There's nothing to worry about – look, I'll talk to my colleagues at the dermatology clinic and visit as soon as – Elizana?'

But I had put down the receiver. I could not move my eyes from the portrait above the mantelpiece, that hideous portrait of her with her loose blue dress and disfigured visage. I felt the distortions on my cheeks, my nose, my brow – and saw them reflected terribly, miserably, *perfectly* in hers. The apothecary had only confirmed my terror. She was inside me – and now she was coming out. She plunged the toadstone ring in the pot of tea – she had to make sure, held it in long and deep to make certain it was safe. Pulling out her wet and leafy hand, she felt the stone rattle louder than it ever had before; in fact it appeared to have eroded, its once smooth surface eaten away like a tiny waning moon. But she didn't seem to notice. She splashed the witch hazel tea over the grotesque mutations of her face, feeling it sting, feeling it burn; still she doused herself in bitter brew, feeling the bones of her fingers lock with spasm, feeling her screaming skin become squamous and numb, swelling and hardening like a fatal allergic response. She could barely stand upright as she staggered into the kitchen. Water, she thought – she needed cold water. Her fused fingers could not operate the tap, and she almost collapsed through the back door into the garden, pressing her face to the earth for the balm of its moisture. Now at the side of the pond she could barely breathe. She could see the ugly shape of the big brown fish lurking just beneath the surface, wallowing in rank mephitic slime, gulping like inverted laughter silent and evil from its prehistoric jaws. She thrust her face into the stagnant water – blessed relief; feeling it seal her scaly skin, numb the agony of her metamorphosis. And like a sorceress she sank – and swam.

# THE CULT OF THE SKULL

There is a certain assemblage of characteristics, thought Dr. Hugog, that a gentleman might possess in such proportions as to veritably guarantee his moonlighting as a broadsheet horoscopist. And nowhere might such characteristics be found in greater concentrations than at the Society for Amateur Anthropologists, in the closing reception of whose annual conference he was presently loitering with a tumbler of nondescript and apparently ageless whiskey. The characteristics in question were in part so familiar because they had once been his own. Hair as wavy as it was wavering over the threshold of a starched collar. The sort of beard that bears a close resemblance to the single retired toothbrush, native to the cupboard beneath the sink, that spends its golden years removing flecks of rust from brass oilcans or grime from old coppers. The adornment – be it badge, brooch or tiepin, collar-clip or cufflink – designed at once to overstate its wearer's eccentricity, and to understate their faculties of good taste. Dr. Hugog, a lifelong amateur anthropologist and indeed the distinguished speaker of the evening, presented a climaxed variant of the phenotype: long hair tied back at the nape, grey beard wild to the point of wisdom, lapel-trinket (often hypertrophied in younger specimens) utterly vestigial – and to top it all off, he hadn't written a horoscope in a decade. He took a sip of warm ice with a hint of peat. He wondered, if one were to compile the astrological acumen of the entire lobby, subtracting only the effects of the open-bar reception, whether the resulting prognosis would be in any way more accurate than that of any single horoscopist amongst them. And if all the competing broadsheets were to independently publish identical prognoses, would it somehow improve their likelihood of coming to pass – indeed, would anyone even notice the coincidence? Probably not, in all cases. Dr. Hugog decided that this snatch of whimsey would serve for an opening gambit with the young anthropologist who had woven through the crowd to meet him.

'Dr. Hugog', said the gentleman, extending his hand, 'Dr. Hugog, that was a wonderful lecture, thank you. Really quite sterling material. I have followed your work with interest – my name is Casimir, Owain Casimir'. Dr. Hugog stooped to shake his hand, although the fellow was of quite ordinary stature. Dr. Hugog stooped to shake everyone's hand, for he was unusually tall; a hereditary condition of the glands which also compelled him to walk with the aid of a stick. His peers considered the resulting air of gravitas a welcome side-effect. 'The pleasure is mine', he replied, 'but say – and I'm afraid you'll just have to indulge me here – how well do you know your astrology?' Happily for Dr. Hugog, antiquarians flock to an 'indulge me' like pedants to a split infinitive. 'Astrology?' asked the younger man, 'you mean, the mansions of the moon and all that?' 'Yes' 'Not very well, I'm afraid'. 'Never cast a horoscope have you – or at least whipped one up for the fish-wrappers?' 'I can't say I have'. 'How unusual', said the doctor, for Owain Casimir appeared, in all other respects, the type specimen of his thesis. In all other respects, perhaps, save one: for it was a mark of uncommon peculiarity to wear one's hat indoors, even amongst antiquarians.

The young gentleman was on the cusp of forming some academic query, but at this point Dr.

Hugog had already detected in him the sort of intellectual enthusiasm that could only mean trouble and was committed to steering the conversation far away from the evening's lecture and (if he could help it) all anthropological matters whatsoever. The ability to perform this manoeuvre reliably is one of the highest social advantages conferred by an eccentric reputation. 'I say – that is a very fine brooch you have there…' he grimaced, affably enough, and asked after its significance. A sure strategy for diversion. Dr. Hugog was confident that not a single person in this room was impervious to the allure of exposition, particularly where it pertained to some personal artefact, which, for amateurs at both, was as close as real life ever came to anthropology. He only needed to make the fellow's story last until he had finished his drink, which would give him an excuse to leave for the bar, and there find convenient distraction in the renewed acquaintance with some distant colleague, freshly made old friend, or long-lost and entirely fictitious sibling. Pleasantly surprised, Casimir tugged at his lapel. The brooch in question was, as they go, rather subtle: a small bronze cruciform with the simple icon of a human head at its base. Had the doctor noticed this detail, he would surely have pursued another avenue of discussion. But tonight was not to be his night. For the human head had been both the subject of Dr. Hugog's

longstanding fascination and his lecture that evening
– and would no doubt be the theme of whatever
cleverness the young anthropologist had intended to
spring on him all along.

'Oh, I'm rather chuffed you noticed. It's a
theological symbol – right up your street, actually.
Origenes, I think, believed that the crucifixion of
Jesus happened to occur exactly where the skull of
the first man Adam was buried. The cross itself
becomes a sort of inverted Tree of Knowledge or
something of that order – a perfect emblem for our
little Society, isn't it? Anyway, I'm glad you noticed,
doctor. I was actually meaning to follow up on your
rather excellent lecture on the theme...'

It is now perhaps expedient to relate that old
'Headhunter' Hugog's period was the earlier pre-
pottery Neolithic, centring on regions of upper
Mesopotamia, while his particular area of research
concerned that mysterious matrix of beliefs and
ritual practises referred to collectively as the Cult of
the Skull. It appears that the bones of the human
head were revered as a sort of naturally occurring
idol during this period, frequently subject to
exhumation, ritual adornment, and secondary burial.
In what was speculated to be a form of ancestor-
worship, many of these skulls had their vital
lineaments reconstructed in layers of clay – evidently
some likeness to the visage they once possessed was

intended, and, at least within the images that had flickered from the doctor's magic lantern that evening, was powerfully if crudely achieved. Yet still more tantalising to the audience of amateur anthropologists (whose weakness for a grand narrative of any kind was legendary) was the unveiling of Dr. Hugog's map of distributions. Newly populated with data from nearly two dozen recent digs, it had implied a remarkable trend: that the Cult of the Skull enjoyed a far greater global range than was previously suspected. Indeed, one of the best-preserved specimens of Dr. Hugog's lecture had been excavated from a cave site as far west as Spain, though in stratigraphic depth it seemed to correlate perfectly with the quintessential Levantine exempla of eight to ten thousand BCE. In the true fashion of the untenured enthusiast, Dr. Hugog was yet to seek publication for his findings, which promised to send shockwaves through his academic field, fallow as it was – and as such, an ill-timed quibble from some critical-thinking non-horoscopist like Owain Casimir would be a dangerous thing. But this was in no measure the younger man's purpose.

'Go on' said Dr. Hugog, whose cordial air was now perceptibly tinctured with the wormwood of weariness. 'It's less of a query, actually – more of a proposal'. This was unusual. 'And what is it that you propose?'. The young man smiled behind his wiry brown moustache. 'I believe I am on the edge of a discovery highly pertinent to your studies, Dr. Hugog – and would profit immensely from your expertise'. It would be ever so easy to dismiss such a claim: a neophyte's grasping for a coat-tail to swing into scholarship. The doctor's own coat-tails were positively ragged with the wear of lesser hands and shorter statures. But just as any member of his creed would have done, Dr. Hugog heard, and respected, his fellow's unspoken injunction – 'indulge me'. The whiskey shivered as he put his glass down. 'A discovery regarding the Cult of the Skull?'. 'Let me explain. I believe I am on the cusp of revealing evidence that the Cult extended as far as the British Isles – and that it had a presence here stronger than anything previously imagined. That it may even have originated-' 'Originated, not likely. Convergent evolution is always a likelihood – especially when it comes to symbology so universal as the human skull. But I am getting ahead of us both. What "evidence" might you possibly possess in support of such a theory?' Casimir collected himself. 'During your lecture, doctor, I noticed that your distribution map presented no data for Neolithic Cult activity in the British Isles'. 'Of course – no dig has been attempted so far from its Mesopotamian cradle. It was only through the fortunate accident of independent finds that I came to direct my researches into Europe, and uncover the pattern I have illustrated tonight'. 'What if I was to tell you–' the younger man ploughed onwards, 'that I have recently inherited a rather special portion of Irish land, on the border of county Meath and Kildare, that I am almost positive contains evidence of Skull Cult activity, a portion of land so far untouched by archaeology – and which, if you are willing, I would dearly enjoin your assistance to excavate. My area of research concerns the souterrain structures that litter the east of that country – and I have come to think, thanks in part to your diligent research, that they too might have some relation to the pre-religious Cult of the Skull'.

Dr. Hugog was, for a moment, impassive. The activity of the drinks reception was beginning to die down, a fellow with a rather parasitic relationship with his suit reached to clap him on the shoulder and offered cursory congratulations before heading out. 'You know', he turned back to his interlocutor, 'I have roots in those parts'. 'I do know' returned Casimir, 'it is, in fact, one of the many reasons I thought you might be interested'. 'How?' 'How what?' 'How did you know?' Casimir smiled. 'I must say I knew something of your ancestry the moment I shook your hand. Some of the very old folk in my Grandfather's village – it is his land that now stands in my name, you see – had hands very much like yours, although nowadays they are seldom seen'. Dr.

Hugog was bemused. He did have slightly unusual hands, that was true, with the four fingers long and nearly equal in length – although such abnormal developments were nothing more than a symptom of his glandular condition. But he would not be an amateur anthropologist if he was not disposed to forgive such extravagant ratiocinations. And besides, the offer was exceedingly tempting. He knew nothing of his heritage; his family had died when he was young, and he had long ago lost the last smatterings of Meath Gaelic they had taught him as a boy. Perhaps they would return to him with the landscape – to say nothing of Owain Casimir's promise of revolutionary evidence for the diasporic Cult of the Skull.

'Is there a date set for the dig, Mr. Casimir?' asked Dr. Hugog. It was strangely difficult to discern whether a lupine or an ovine aspect predominated the younger man's countenance. 'The ferry sails on Friday' he said. 'Friday? You mean Friday overmorrow?' 'Yes. I apologise profusely for the invitation at such short notice – although I am very glad indeed to have crossed paths with you tonight. I do hope you can accommodate a few weeks' sojourn – I would sorely miss your expertise, and need hardly stress that the opportunity is not to be scoffed at. That land is crammed with mysteries, if the rural lore is any indication; mysteries no-one has been able to investigate, until now, that is, until us'. Dr. Hugog cursed inwardly. Though the years had not yet leeched the pigment from his whiskers, this Casimir was not unblooded in the field of antiquarian mesmerism. How could that same intellectual enthusiasm which portended so much trouble when levelled at himself be so very persuasive with an inverse trajectory?

'Your offer is very kind', began Dr. Hugog. Under any other circumstance he would not hesitate to join forces with a fellow amateur in the spontaneous pursuit of some wild paleohistorical goose. Such things, like north walls, had way of yielding strange fruit. Yet in this case, two factors gave him pause – two chaotic variables for which, before now, he had never had cause to account. The first was that this address to the Society for Amateur Anthropologists had been intended – with its comprehensive display of erudition and dazzling results – for a sort of grand conclusion, a billet-doux and adieu to a lifetime well-spent in understanding the Cult of the Skull. It would serve as prelude for the decisive publication that would bookend the great 'Headhunter' Hugog's advancements in the field, and most importantly, it would give him the freedom to break new ground elsewhere.

The second factor concerned a particular patch of new ground that yearned for attention, if not, in this case, the archaeologist's wonted brush and trowel. For Dr. Hugog had, in his old age, become a father. Having spent his whole life a natural bachelor, it would certainly have surprised his fellows at the Society for Amateur Anthropologists to learn of Dr. Hugog's most unexpected discovery in the field of human sciences, pending official classification but tentatively identified as love. Alzada Stormonth was herself an anthropologist of resolutely amateur persuasions, though principally a newspaper typist responsible for setting the daily astrological column. They had met at a Society reception, incidentally, under bizarrely similar circumstances to those in which he presently found himself. He had thought she looked like a horoscopist, and she had thought – based on the accuracy of his prediction – that he was himself not inexperienced in the matter. The typical flights of fancy ensued, she had accompanied him to the cave sites of Spain, and to the couple's mutual surprise their return coincided with the birth of dear Henry, now eight months old. Regrettably, Dr. Hugog's scholarly obsessions had already deprived him of much of his young son's company. Now that he had finally presented his findings, he desired very much to return home and make up for his absence during this crucial period, latterly made still more crucial by the unfortunate revelation that Henry had inherited his father's glandular condition and would need special care for his frailty. It was thought that Dr. Hugog's age was a contributing factor for its transmission. It goes without question that all this amounted to a rather substantial feeling of guilt behind the doctor's aloof, eccentric carapace – a feeling he was loath to compound by breaking his promise to Alzada and abandoning Henry for another month, all in the name of indulging yet another whim…

The hotel lobby was empty now. Dr. Hugog hadn't heard the last members leaving. Owain Casimir stood there, waiting patiently, eyes bright with promise. 'I think I shall take you up on it', finished the tall man, and he wrapped his long fingers strangely around the other's hand.

***

The day was dreary and the ferry trip uneventful. He had met Casimir at the docks that morning and they had boarded together, stowing their not inconsiderable mass of combined equipment and spending the crossing mostly beneath the grey clouds on deck. The younger man kept opening conversations that Dr. Hugog would, without really even meaning to, summarily close. He had disappointed his family – yes, and it *was* a family. For decades he had no-one to disappoint but himself. Alzada had been quietly miserable since the moment he divulged his plans to leave. He knew she shared his belief in the allure of discovery, and what was worse, he could not help but concede to her evaluation that its present costs were excessive. Yet it had been Henry's reaction that really pained his old heart. He hadn't seen the boy for a stretch of weeks as he finalised his plans for the conference, and expected very much to greet him in an embrace of mutual delight upon returning home. He had knocked a whimsical rhythm with the head of his cane. The answering rhythm of footfalls, the opening of the door – and there was Alzada, with Henry cocooned in her arms. Sweeping in, he leant over to take the pale boy, only to find him in a state of pitiful agitation. At the age of eight months, his faculty of speech was uncommonly precocious – 'no, no, no', he had cried. 'Is anything the matter?' he asked Alzada, who, as mediator, was better accustomed to both the mystifying ways of infants and the scatterbrained impotence of antiquarians. That was when Henry had made his second utterance. It might have been the fortuitous coincidence of a nascent wail with a bubble of breath, but to Dr. Hugog, it sounded uncannily like the plaintive words 'don't go'. Don't go! The prescient power of infants never ceased to astonish him. He had just walked in at the door and already his son could sense his imminent departure. Some fellows of the Society for Amateur Anthropologists had once been very interested in undertaking a cross-cultural survey of maternal-telepathic phenomena. Dr. Hugog wondered whether there might not also be a phenomenon of paternal telepathy. Henry, who hadn't even a single winter to his grain, had done a better job of seeing into his grey inscrutable head than throngs of doctorate supervisors and even fellow amateurs had been – perhaps even better than the fellow sitting opposite, whose tongue was as sharp as his eye and vice-versa. 'Don't go', his son had told him, 'don't go' – and yet, here he was. Erroneous judgements were characteristic of Dr. Hugog's lifestyle and scholarly praxis, where they were often and paradoxically committed to his profit. Like outliers on some Nornic graph, he could do nothing but pray that destiny would continue to follow the scientific method and reward their diligent investigation.

'The local name for the mound is Gogoth's Tump', said Casimir, although Dr. Hugog wasn't certain whether he was broaching new conversation or continuing with some prior spiel. 'Clearly a corruption of the Hebrew 'Golgotha', the place of the skull – or Calvary, hence the brooch'. The doctor demurred. 'Flimsy evidence for the migration of a Skull Cult originating in the Middle East, one would think. A local name is a devilish thing, as any folklorist will tell you'. The younger man laughed. 'Oh no, I suggest nothing of the sort. If anything, the biblical etymology is owing to the area's early Christian history. It is said that in the fifth century – long after the introduction of any Cult activity, to be sure – St. Brigid founded one of the most important Christian outposts in Celtic Ireland, Cill Dara, the Church of the Oak, whence 'Kildare', on whose borderlands my family have lived for generations' – 'and where you intend for us to open up this "Gogoth's Tump", so nebulously entangled with my area of study?' 'Precisely'. The men continued their halting exchange as they disembarked the ferry, collected their gear, and bundled into a carriage. Squat villages rolled past, moss in their gables and slates in their walls. Holts and shaws sped by in smears of muddy green. The sky was the colour and texture of a runaway bellwether, and grim mizzle hung in the air like a faerie phalanx, redoubting on the grass of the hills and the hawthorn brakes of country lanes. It was early evening by the time the carriage stopped threading the twist of dirt roads and trackless pasture, and Dr. Hugog's thorough disorientation was balanced only by the acute certainty of his utter remoteness from civilisation. The balding crowns of each autumn oak, silhouetted against the sky, looked for all the world like the lateral cross-sections of a human brain, vessels connecting each dark cluster of detail, preserved between glass for the pleasure of some cosmic microscopist. Unloading his things from the carriage, Dr. Hugog noticed his companion swill the crisp air like fine homebrew. He discretely did the same, filtering the damp atmosphere through his beard. Though he knew he had returned to the place of his forbears, he could not say that he felt any sort of belonging, any sort of spiritual connection. The air tasted rather like the whiskey he had ordered at the Society reception – an empty celebration for the work that was evidently not yet complete. 'Come on', said Casimir, 'the farmhouse is a short walk away. Let's find a path to help you with that stick. No – don't worry yourself, I've got the luggage'.

Even in the gathering darkness it was clear that the farmhouse was a rather dilapidated affair. Rounding a thicket at its threshold, Dr. Hugog was at once surprised to see a figure leaning against a fencepost, stocky and ragged, swaddled in a drab motheaten jumper and a wild white beard damp with rain. The minute his companion caught sight of him, he dropped the luggage with a cry of delight, and shrugging off his backpack ran to greet the apparition. Dr. Hugog winced as his archaeological instruments clattered in the mud, though his expression quickly shaded into perplexity as he beheld the passion with which Owain Casimir clasped the scruffy old man to his breast, lavishing his face with kisses in a devotional rapture of which the object only seemed but half aware. The pair embraced for a full five minutes before Casimir pulled away, wiping tears of affection from his eyes. 'Oh sorry – sorry, Dr. Hugog, sorry – you will pardon my high emotions, please – this is my grandfather, Tundale. We call him the Druid. He remembered I was coming! He waited for us here – Grandfather, this is my friend, Dr. Hugog. His ancestors lived here! He will be our guest'. 'Alton. It is a pleasure to meet you, sir'. The old man smiled benignly back. 'Let's get you inside, Grandfather – what have I told you about going outside without a hat, especially in weather like this? Dr. Hugog, help me with the bags – yes, that's it, back to the farmhouse. It is such a joy to see you again, Grandfather…'

Even while removing his own hat and ducking a full foot and a half, Dr. Hugog still managed to scalp himself on the upper frame of the farmhouse door. 'Watch yourself' cautioned Casimir, as he bustled to wrap a fleece around his grandfather's shoulders, and, taking a ragged flat-cap from a peg, placed it smartly on the old man's hoary noll. What an unusual custom these Casimirs have, thought Dr. Hugog, to wear one's hat indoors – and being the consummate anthropologist he was, replaced his own headgear. It would not trouble him while seated. Owain put some logs in the fireplace and set it smouldering, and soon the three of them were warm and settled around a table on which stood a loaf of black bread and a hunk of hard, woody-coloured cheese. They ate while the young man explained everything to his grandfather, who smiled blankly. Dr. Hugog cracked off a heel of bread – it was rather stale – and crumbled a shard of cheese between his teeth. 'Tomorrow we are going to begin digging at Gogoth's Tump, Grandfather' Owain said with quite incongruous levity. Dr. Hugog did not like the slightly too loud and clipped quality his voice assumed when talking to the elderly gentleman. There was a fine line between care and condescension – with his frailty and his walking-staff he had watched people attempt to navigate it for much of his adulthood. Then something quite unexpected happened. For the first time since their paths had crossed, the Druid began to speak. His voice was thin, wheedling and entirely undirected, and with such a bale of dead sphagnum muffling his jowls, the effect was eerily ventriloquistic. 'Gogoth's Tump?' he seemed to say, and Dr. Hugog strained to decipher his brogue, 'where auld Christian folks did paganny sacrifices?'. Owain Casimir put his arm on his grandfather's shoulder and laughed. 'Oh, those old stories! I was telling Dr. Hugog here all about the old legends on our ferry ride over – isn't that right, doctor?' Dr. Hugog could not remember hearing anything about sacrifices, and smiled cordially. 'Right, I think that'll do us for tonight' continued Casimir, 'Grandfather, begging your pardon, I need to show Dr. Hugog to his chambers'. The tall man stood up and narrowly missed a low beam to the temple. It was as though a tower had charged towards a battering ram and feinted at the last moment. 'Thank you ever so much for your hospitality, Mr. Casimir' he said to the Druid, who returned his courtesy with a placid smile, but withheld an answering 'goodnight' as the doctor followed his associate out of the room.

Dr. Hugog sidestepped a leak in the hallway's ceiling. 'Pardon me for asking, Mr. Casimir – but is your grandfather quite well?' He was being led the way they had entered the farmhouse. 'I've arranged for you to stay in a little outhouse, if that's alright – I could not vouch for, well, the *safety* of any of the guestrooms, and besides I suspect you'll find the additional privacy to your scholarly advantage'. Casimir showed the doctor to a rather wretched looking hovel not far from the farmhouse grounds, and fishing in his pocket, gave him a key like a squirrel's jawbone. 'As for Grandfather – I love him dearly, but the poor man suffered a mental aberration many moons ago, and the corrective operation did not go quite as planned. He's a lobotomite. He's still all there, mostly – some of the time'. Dr. Hugog faltered. 'I'm very sorry to hear that'. 'It's quite alright', replied the other man with a passing note of sadness, 'it is owing to his condition that I was able to claim my inheritance prematurely – including legal ownership of this very land we tread. Tomorrow I'll show you Gogoth's Tump, and we can begin making plans for excavation. I am sure it won't disappoint'. 'Thank you, Mr. Casimir, for your generosity'. 'It's quite alright', the other man said again, and they bade each other goodnight.

Inside the hovel was cramped and cobwebbed. There was a writing desk stocked with candles, a slightly rotten chair, and a bed much too minimal for Dr. Hugog's lofty proportions. The geometry of the roof was such that it funnelled the night wind to a ghostly wail. But at least there were no leaks, and a lock on the door, and setting down his cane Dr. Hugog soon found himself descending into a dull, leaden slumber.

***

There is nothing quite like a splash of cold water to remind one of the skull beneath one's skin. Dr. Hugog felt the planes and angles of his face stand out with graven severity as he washed himself over the tin basin of water that Casimir had drawn from the well. He raked a spindly hand through his beard, shaking out the cold droplets like snow from a grey cloud. Back when he was naïve and ambitious – back when he had earned his doctorate – he had known a colleague at the Faculty of Anthropology so proficient that he could extrapolate a muscular structure from a bone structure and so produce a sketched portrait of any known hominin species within the hour to an exceptional degree of accuracy. At that moment, Dr. Hugog, shivering from the cold, felt like he could probably manage a self-portrait from identical principles. It was very fortunate that his pre-pottery Neolithic subjects had done most of the work themselves, remoulding the living features onto the skull out of clay, occasionally substituting a river pebble for an eyeball, a small shell for a tooth. It was with this thought fresh in his mind that Dr. Hugog packed his equipment and prepared to follow Owain Casimir to a distant acre of the property, excited in spite of his still-lingering guilt to unearth some new understanding of the Cult of the Skull.

'Why do they call your grandfather the Druid?' he asked as they walked. Casimir smiled. 'It's a sort of pun, I suppose, on the Church of the Oak – 'Druid', of course, coming from 'duir', oak, same root as 'Dara'. He's been called it his entire life, growing up in Kildare. Of course he also had some funny ideas, growing up. They got to him in the end, I think'. The pair went on in silence, and Dr. Hugog inwardly cursed the waning of the old tongue. They passed a few small dig sites, half overgrown with weeds – these were the souterrains of Casimir's research. Generally assumed to have served as storehouses or storm shelters, the young anthropologist could not fathom precisely why their frequency seemed to increase with proximity to the mound, and was enthusiastically proposing some ritual functionality or other as Dr. Hugog's eyes slid keenly over the damp green topography, snarled here and there with windblown hawthorn and tumbledown cairns. A hillock approached them. It was unmissable, an almost grotesque bulge in the nigh-featureless expanse. It could be nothing other than Gogoth's Tump.

The mound was a rather large one. An average walker might cross its diameter in thirty strides, Dr. Hugog in twenty. It was shaggy with unkempt grass, and at its topmost point, strange to say, stood the scraggy armature of an adolescent tree, long dead. Dr. Hugog had seen his fair share of barrows both opened and unhatched, and could tell at a glance that Gogoth's Tump was without question the product of some ancient artifice. Might indeed the Cult of the Skull have achieved some foothold here? He followed Owain Casimir around the circumference of the mound. The younger man was saying there had been a rabbit hole or somesuch opening that might productively be widened into a lateral tunnel – but Dr. Hugog was lost in thought. He had not felt so upon his arrival, nor indeed at the Casimir farmhouse, where the prevailing emotion was, speaking frankly, a kind of vague disquietude. But here at Gogoth's Tump, he had been struck by a profound sense of connection, of homecoming. Dr. Hugog had great faith in his sense of intuition. Perhaps that too had been passed down to his dear little teething oracle. In that moment, however, the sense was very strong. He knew that Casimir had not led him astray on some fanciful escapade of the amateur imaginary. Here, instead, he would learn something of the Cult of the Skull; he would find answers to those manifold sleepless questions that haunted him precisely because they had yet to be bound in language or shape.

I shall not bore you with the soporific minutiae of the anthropologist's plans, the initial excavation of their tunnel nor the quarrelsome issue of its structural support. All such details may doubtless be found in Dr. Hugog's notebook, whose ambient reek of tallow derives from its owner's unfailing habit of recording them in the nocturnal solitude of his hovel. It was on the third or fourth day of digging, however, that the first real discovery was made. Owain Casimir noticed it first – and with unconcealed delight, extricated one of the objects from its cloddish matrix. Dr. Hugog beheld it with the rising vertigo common to all antiquarian souls found teetering on the verge of discovery. It was a globose mineral artefact somewhat smaller than his enclosed fist; its upwards-facing surface graven with a stellate glyph, organically wrought and much too delicate for the undexterous chisels of early men. 'A shepherd's crown' said Dr. Hugog, marvelling softly. 'We call them pixie loaves here', replied Casimir. These fossilised sea-urchins were not uncommonly unearthed from barrows across the British Isles, sometimes in great profusion, even far inland. It was speculated that the unusual pattern at the apex of the urchin's dome resembled a sun-ring and so possessed talismanic properties – certainly, the pre-Celtic association of such fossils with the afterlife was well attested and still present among superstitious folk of the chalky downs. But it was not the rarity of the find that excited the doctor. It was the principle. For this naturally-occurring talisman represented an identical ascription of ritual semiotics to biological relics as the ancient Cult of the Skull.

It was not long before the next pixie loaf emerged from the flank of the mound, and it very soon became apparent that the men had struck a rich seam of the talismanic objects, a constellation of runic stars all facing the sky. At the point of this find, it was decided to extend the lateral diameter of the tunnel (now six feet deep into the flank of the hill). The conclusion was inescapable, that Gogoth's Tump was completely ringed about with many hundreds of these bizarre offerings. It was a major breakthrough in the expedition, for it indicated, among other things, the certainty of further treasures within. Dr. Hugog felt his doubts evaporating. Even if this barrow was entirely unconnected with the Cult of the Skull, the extraordinary care and opulence evidenced by the preparation of this stratum marked it as a site of great anthropological importance. It could only be seen as a high honour and a privilege to have played so central a role in its discovery. Alzada of all people would have to understand, and Henry would doubtless come around to it too, when he was old enough.

The next days were spent in detailed sketching and cataloguing of the artefact-rich band. It was decided that a section of the pixie-loaf ring approximately five feet in length would be removed to facilitate inward extension of the tunnel, in the hope that any further deposits would be situated on the same horizontal plane. It was not long until their suspicions proved correct. Digging had slowed for fear of damaging any sensitive objects, but it was only a foot or two further into the mound that Dr.

Hugog's eye settled on a very peculiar piece of debris. He had taken it initially for a large shepherd's crown, dislodged by geological processes from the actually quite regular orbit of the others. He tried it with his brush, but the clotted earth yielded nothing to its bristles. He began to work around it – and as he did, it soon became clear that it could be no such thing. For a start, it was fragmented. The appearance of roundness was sustained only by the crush of its surrounding terrain. Dr. Hugog's heart played the bones on his ribcage. He had been here before. He abandoned his tools and felt the slither of damp clay on his fingers as they slowly, painstakingly eased the object out of the earth. It disengaged with a sharp squelch. Before he had even revolved it in his hands, the doctor knew what he was looking at. Its negative-space impression stared back at him from the tunnel clay. It was the ancient, jawless skull of an infant.

That the remains of children should feature in Skull Cult practises was not entirely unheard of. Dr. Hugog had himself many years ago excavated a specimen in a Levantine temple complex, thought to have belonged to a young hierodule or temple slave. But it was very rare – and such fragile remains were seldom as well preserved as this. The doctor contemplated the almost alien bone structure of the paedomorphic skull: the wishbonelike architecture of the zygomatic arch, tiny and miraculously intact, the huge orbits of its eyes, the bulbous braincase whose sundered plates resembled potsherds in the clay. He felt a twinge of some strange new instinct – and swiftly suppressed it with a shout to Owain Casimir, who was sketching atop the mound. He descended damp with drizzle, a stray curl beneath his hat and a dewdrop sparkle in his eye. 'How old do you think it is?' he asked Dr. Hugog after a while. The doctor's brow furrowed. 'Probably Celtic to judge by its situation in this mound, with the shepherd's crowns. It's hard to make a stratigraphic estimate because of the structure's elevation. If it's related in any way to the Cult of the Skull – which I'm not saying it is – it could be even older, though its remarkably well preserved, so perhaps a last vestige of its pre-Celtic decadence. The end of the Stone Age in the British Isles, would you agree? I should like to get it sent to London for chemical assessment'. Mr. Casimir smiled grimly. 'I meant, how old do you think *they were*?'.

With two men working at the excavation, the tunnel widened considerably as it grew deeper. Very soon another object came up – then another, then another. Soon several rows of tiny skulls stared up at them from the wet grass, gormless and infantile, in various conditions of decay. Not a single brainpan was intact. Dr. Hugog felt uneasy. He had never before seen anything like this. It was not the vast preponderance of infant remains; ossuaries and mass graves were relatively common in his line of study. It was the fact that clearly none of these infants – of whom only the skulls had been unearthed – were the *subjects* of the burial monument. While clearly not as numerous, it was evident that the skulls were almost certainly arranged in a concentric circle within that of the shepherd's crowns. They too were but accoutrements to some ancient, charnel ceremony.

Daylight was shrinking and the persistent drizzle seemed as if it would gather momentum. 'Dr. Hugog, you will forgive my suggestion – are we not here looking at unquestionable evidence for the Cult of the Skull? This arrangement is plainly ritual – the remains, no doubt symbolic'. 'It's a common symbol' said Hugog curtly. 'Skull worship has arisen in many places, in many times. I see no evidence that this… site is in any way connected to the Mesopotamian manifestation. Besides, I have seen nothing like this in all of my research. We've stumbled upon something profound, that's for sure – but you will forgive my hesitation in drawing such swift conclusions'. The younger man sat next to Dr. Hugog, who was stooping his great height in the shelter of the tunnel. Brown rainwater dribbled from its mouth. 'But what if… what if that's precisely the point. Come, come, Dr. Hugog! Where's all that daring eccentricity? Just imagine – might we not be sitting at the Cult's global epicentre, from which all lesser branches diverge? You said for yourself that you weren't sure how old this all was. Neolithic, perhaps – why not Mesolithic? The land-bridge would have made for convenient transmission of ideas east across the continent...' 'Enough, Mr. Casimir – let us not exceed ourselves. I'll believe it when I see it'. 'But I think I've already seen it. Let me ask you an odd question, Dr. Hugog, but indulge me – how are we sure that those infant skulls even belonged to *homo sapiens*?'.

Dr. Hugog lingered at Gogoth's Tump that evening while Mr. Casimir headed back to help his grandfather with supper. He said he had to gather his tools and make a few final notes *in situ* – but he really just wanted to ponder. Having crawled out of the cramped tunnel, Dr. Hugog slowly mounted the barrow with the aid of his stick, and slumped against the stunted tree. Tilting his head up, he tried to keep his eyes open as raindrops jolted against the nerves of his face or burrowed into his beard. A withered grey leaf spiralled in the wind, identifying his dysfunctional shelter as a travestied oak. Soon Dr. Hugog was looking outwards, surveying the vaporous landscape by the last glimmer of fading light. It was not quite as featureless as he had first thought. Indeed, where he had snagged his walking-cane in the approach of the mound that morning was a slight convexity in the grass. It was flanked at a distance by others in a wide arc, some of which were less reticent to display their nature. They were the low-cut stumps of ancient trees, reclaimed almost entirely by the earth. As Dr. Hugog swivelled his head, he saw that the stumps formed a perfect circle, and he was in the centre of it. He shivered. Oaks too, no doubt. He had read of the druid groves – and thought of Casimir's strange, pottering grandfather, and what he had muttered about long-ago sacrifices. The rain was slowly washing the clay from the skulls they had unearthed and left in the grass. Dr. Hugog suddenly felt the intense desire to leave that place. Cold and utterly sodden, he shifted his towering frame towards the farmhouse and slowly departed, stick feeling the slippery ground for hidden roots.

When he arrived, Casimir was nowhere to be seen. Dr. Hugog surmised that his colleague had retired early to journal the queer ideas of the day, as he had occasionally been known to do. He was thankful for the courtesy of stew left in the cauldron above the fireplace and a haunch of hard bread on the table. What with his attention split between the deduction of these arrangements and the delicate navigation of his head beneath the murderously low and gloomy ceiling, it was hardly surprising that Dr. Hugog failed to notice the Druid sitting in the corner, quietly mumbling to himself – and very surprising when he did. He winced as his skull scraped the underside of an upstairs floorboard. The Druid barely looked up from beneath his motheaten cap, and continued mumbling what sounded to Dr. Hugog like some sort of prayer. His coarse hands clutched at a rosary – no, some other pendant, dimly visible in the flickering glow of the fireplace, and Dr. Hugog was oddly mortified to recognise a small bronze cruciform with the icon of a human head at its base. 'Mr. Casimir-' he began, to very little effect. The old man continued staring and mumbling, though he called his name two or three times more. 'Tundale, sir, please – tell me, if at all you know – were *children* ever sacrificed at Gogoth's Tump?' The Druid looked up. 'Gogoth's Tump?' 'Yes, Gogoth's Tump!' 'Where good Christian folks spilt heatheny blood'. Dr. Hugog let the strangeness of that particular mytheme slip. 'But heathen *children*? We found skulls, Mr. Casimir, infant skulls – split open at the top like eggshells…' He forced himself to stay collected, forced himself to assume the receptive conviviality of the immersion anthropologist stranded in some distant land – 'do you know anything about this, Mr. Casimir? Do you remember any old stories?'. The Druid thumbed his curious periapt and shrugged his beard in an occulted smile. His eyes had the sort of pallor only found in visionaries and cataracts. And then he spoke, his words chilling the old doctor to his spindled bones. 'While a baby's head is still soft, still open… it can see the things usually kept hid from us mortals.'

But whether the Druid had more to say on the matter, Dr. Hugog would never know – for he had doffed his hat, and seizing the hunk of bread from the table, departed to the outhouse. The Druid's resumed mumbles echoed in his ears until he turned the key behind him. He had to write a letter home – to his beloved Alzada, to his dearest Henry. He had betrayed them both. A damp match gave a ratcheting hiss as it sprung to feeble life, kissing the wick of a maggot-coloured candle whose waxen plinth oozed into the grain of the writing desk. Those skulls they had found in such great numbers were so young that their cranial plates had not yet fused – they could have been as young as Henry was. And what was it again that his son had told him – 'don't go?' Don't go! Dr. Hugog wrote and wrote, the letters uncoiling like webwork from the spinnerets of his spidery hand. He begged forgiveness for his rashness and his folly, he confessed such love for his family as had previously been reserved for his scholarship alone – he promised to curtail his expedition and return as soon as humanely possible. For that evening Dr. Hugog had glimpsed, in a moment of yawning terror, the veracity of the Druid's assertion. He should have trusted his son's clairvoyance. But more than this, he saw how such people – such children, whose minds were open to those inscrutable influences that rebounded from the ossified braincases of maturity – were sacred to the Cult of the Skull, or at least to whichever debased form it took in this remote Irish nowhere. He sealed the letter and scrawled an address. Casimir could send it next time he went into Kildare for supplies. Dr. Hugog knew, as he had known all along, that had made a grievous mistake – and he knew that he had to atone for it.

***

Over the following days, excavations continued at Gogoth's Tump. Dr. Hugog had not informed his companion that he intended to leave as soon as the dig site was fully mapped – completing the brunt of the analytical work outside their collaboration. Yet Casimir too seemed somewhat hurried – with fervour, perhaps, rather than guilt. The tunnel now bored a good twelve feet into the mound, and, widening as it went, caused a few practical complications; with such a small team, frequent pauses were necessary to fortify its rather improvisational supports. When not engaged in their burrowing, the men took care to record their discoveries in minute detail. Over twenty skulls had emerged, and it was now known for certain that they too formed a ring around the barrow. Dr. Hugog had not mentioned his interaction with the Druid, and was cautious not to emphasise his subsequent theory for their symbolic interment. He had the strong feeling that the inculcation of such a mind as Casimir's with such ideas as those could only bode ill for both his scholarly reputation and his sanity. And since Dr. Hugog's life might fairly have been described as a perennial struggle for the maintenance of both against impossible odds, he would be loath to lose them over a mere spot of overzealous quackery.

'Dr. Hugog! Come over here – look at this'. The doctor scrunched his face in pre-emptive aching. The daily exertions of the dig site in tandem with an undersized bed had not been kind to his rather sensitive skeleton, and it was with considerable gyp that he troubled his great height into the cramped tunnel with Casimir. 'Look', said the younger man, sinking his trowel into the clay. It sunk about an inch and stopped with a dull clink. He tried it again, a little higher, and the result was the same. 'An obstruction?' 'It's got to be massive. Help me clear this dirt'. Very soon the men were scraping through the layer of clay. It was the sort of substrate whose frigid smell never left your throat, nor its dregs your fingernails. It was too dense to accommodate even the knotted catacombs of worms, yet the men plied as if it were their native element, eventually revealing the obstacle to their path. It was a solid surface, apparently of mineral composition, somewhat paler in colour than the surrounding earth. Though the patch they had uncovered was flat, it showed the subtle beginnings of an upwards curvature when more was cleared away. 'There's no getting around this, that's for sure' murmured the doctor. 'I have never seen a barrow with a solid core. What's the point in burying a boulder?' 'I have no clue' said Casimir, whetting his smile on the mystery of it all. 'We're not sure it's completely in the way, are we? We could widen the tunnel, follow its curve. Maybe we'll find another angle through. I've seen a picture of you working a megalith at *Göbekli Tepe,* haven't I? We can do the same. We could even sink another tunnel, if you're willing, to maximise our chances – and catalogue a whole other transect of archaeological data in the process'. 'You think this is a megalithic structure then?' 'What else?' 'I don't know. You're probably right – it must form some part of a subterraneous tomb complex. The rest of this site is so lavishly and meticulously arranged, it can hardly be accidental. But I must confess-', the doctor checked himself, and seeing Casimir's expectant eye, relented, 'well, the calcareous quality and hue of this barrier reminded me somewhat of, well, of Lethbridge's hill-figures. Chalky gods and giants hunkering beneath the Wandlebury soil. It's fanciful,

I know, and clearly this –' he tapped the surface with his trowel, emitting a dull clang – 'is something altogether different. But still. Gogoth's Tump has proved a remarkable site in every respect – and I would not be surprised if this anomaly too had some important ritual purpose'. 'The Cult of the Skull', agreed Casimir. Dr. Hugog chose not to acknowledge him as they set to work rounding the obstacle.

But very soon another impediment to their efforts became apparent. The tunnel had grown so wide at its deepest point that daylight no longer reached the area which the two anthropologists were clearing. Mercifully Casimir had some candles in his satchel, which Dr. Hugog was able to light with a firesteel – though the younger man resolved to travel to the nearest village the following day for some oil-lanterns. Here Dr. Hugog dogeared the mental page. Such a trip would be an excellent opportunity to post his letter. The two laboured onwards by candlelight like archivists in a library of land, making little conversation until Casimir piped up. 'By the gods new and old', he swore, 'Dr. Hugog – did you hear that?' 'Hear what?' 'This'. Owain Casimir struck his trowel against the stony surface of the obstacle – and instead of a dull clink, expressed a resounding echo. 'This isn't some acoustic property of the tunnel, is it?' asked the doctor. 'No – try it yourself, anywhere else.

See? Whatever this object is – it's at least partially hollow'.

Now the magnetism of discovery was undeniable. Dr. Hugog felt very strongly that sense of kinship – that ineffable intuition of belonging he had felt nowhere else in this strange place but Gogoth's Tump. The excitement overrode the pain of his posture, hunched and troglodytic, and reached an adrenal crescendo when his fingers brushed, then curled, then clung to what could be nothing other than an irregularity in the obstacle's surface. He dug and dug away at the damp clay, shivering with the charnel cold – until the anomaly was bare in the candlelight. It was the lip of a fissure – a possible pathway into the barrow? Soon the younger man was helping him excavate all the surrounding earth, following the rim of the crack with hands growing numb, showing it for a cleft, then a gap, then a hole, then a portal: rounded and large enough for a man to crawl through. The anthropologists whooped with joy. 'It's some sort of passage tomb', said Dr. Hugog, 'It has to be. There's no other explanation. Entering the sanctum through this portal, humbled on hands and knees, was meant to represent one's progress to the afterlife, or the otherworld'. The hole was still plugged entirely with clay, but the promise of some hollow space behind it gave the men renewed energy, and they hurried on with their work. Dr. Hugog gasped as his trowel bit into the gummy earth and met emptiness behind. Perhaps he had been wrong to abandon his family for this strange adventure – but at this very moment, he regretted nothing. A gust of stale and ancient air oozed out of the dark opening, extinguishing the candles in their makeshift alcoves. Casimir struggled to relight them as they peered into the gloom, overwhelmed by the sense of unspeakable ancientness that pooled around them, viscous as bitumen or votive honey. While the cavity was almost completely filled with earth and debris, it looked like there was enough space for a single man to enter. 'You do the honours, doctor', grinned Casimir, as he handed him a candle.

It could scarcely be denied that Dr. Hugog, crouched on hands and knees as he crept into the cavity, really did feel like he was crossing the threshold into another world. There was not sufficient space for him to stand erect – but it was clear that there would be enough for both men once the chamber had been fully excavated. 'It's like sitting in some great stoneware pot', marvelled Dr. Hugog, 'it strains the imagination to think how such a thing was done…' 'What do you see?' called Casimir. 'Nothing much, mostly just earth and – and the dangling roots of the oak! No wonder it's such a miserable specimen – starved to death on a chameleon's diet'. The vermiform roots, withered and cracked as the elbows of an elephant, emerged from the ceiling like a brood of necropolitan serpents. 'That means...' began the younger man, 'it's forced its way through this stony integument. So there must be an opening directly at the peak of the mound – an opening that would let in the sunlight! Doctor, hold the fort – I'm going back to the farmhouse for an axe'. 'Are you sure we should-' began Dr. Hugog, but Casimir, in his infinite youth and eagerness, was already halfway out of the tunnel.

Dr. Hugog sat alone in the hollow, bathed in the flickering light of his candle. He had always thought that nearness to ancient structures exerted a peculiar bodily response – almost as if their presence amplified the latent effects of gravity. In this place, under the concentrated pressure of ages, Dr. Hugog felt ready to merge with the clay. He felt entirely autochthonous. With a curious tranquillity, he began to clear earth away from the inner entrance of the barrow sanctum. He brought the candle closer. The more earth he cleared, the more a strange pattern came into focus. At first he took it for a simple discolouration of the mound's inner shell – but the more he scraped away, the more obvious it became. It was chipped and pocked, as if struck by many weapons, but it was unmistakable. He was gazing upon a handprint, or rather a negative hand stencil, of unbelievably primitive design. Trembling, he did as men have done since times immemorial, and placed his own hand over. Its four fingers were long, and nearly equal in length.

\*\*\*

Days came and passed. Dr. Hugog's letter had been taken to the village, and a set of lanterns had returned from it. The shrunken oak atop Gogoth's Tump had been lopped down and its roots pickaxed out of the ground; now a shaft several feet deep filtered a few candles' worth of daylight into the inner cavity of the barrow. After a night of high weather, the anthropologists were disturbed to find that their tunnel had suffered a partial collapse – to Dr. Hugog's chagrin, an additional day was dedicated to widening, straightening and reenforcing the passage into the stony vestibule. More pixie loaves were discovered, three more skulls, and loose cranial plates belonging to several others. With additional space to manoeuvre and a linear path to navigate, it was hoped that emptying the central chamber of accumulated earth would be a comparatively swift and easy process – a process which it was finally time to undertake. He had shown Casimir the handprint, and the promise of more parietal art tantalised both intellects beyond words. Gogoth's Tump was a discovery like no other, and Dr. Hugog had mostly suspended his attempts to unriddle its relationship with the Cult of the Skull. Right now, the sheer novelty of the enigma was overwhelming. Be it Celtic, pre-Celtic, Neolithic or even (as Casimir would have it) far older than that – what mattered now was the raw experience of that which lay within, like the sweet kernel of a nut, or the moral of an olden fable.

The doctor thought of his family while he worked. This could never be his redemption, as he shovelled through centuries of muck, a single letter could never make up for lost time. But he would return with a story to tell, wiser, and older – older, in fact, by thousands and thousands of years, a totality of ancient years experienced only by himself and Owain Casimir – and maybe that would be time enough regained to equal one month lost with his poor, dear, precious son.

The first thing to emerge from the steadily emptying chamber was the suggestion of another entrance. Located on the same side of the cavity, not overly far from the portal through which they had come, was the rounded lip of another opening: rare for passage tombs, but clearly this was no ordinary tomb. 'The processionals, the ritual traffic in and out of this sacred space – must have been enormous, to require two gateways'. 'So you'd think', replied Dr. Hugog, 'but where is the evidence? We haven't come across a single artefact – I've been shovelling pure clay. You'd expect grave-goods at least, wouldn't you – if not grave treasures'. This observation was not strictly true. Casimir had pointed out a dark carbonic stratum, visible in the lantern-light – 'decomposed grain. Ancient wheat or barley, reverted to earth – it's common in souterrains, particularly the older half-buried examples. Ritual offerings can also be perishable'. And there was also the matter of the handprints. Both entrances were surrounded with them – ghostly negatives, sprayed in iron-based pigment. Each was chipped away as if in ritual desecration, the sort of damage, Dr. Hugog thought, he had seen inflicted by primitive hunters upon images of their prey, speeding the success of their hunt through magical sympathy. All seemed to belong to different individuals, to judge by their variations in size, women and children too – yet all bore an uncanny kinship with the proportions of his own. Many people indeed had passed through here, he pondered, leaving nothing but the memory of their touch – and he, of course, was just another pilgrim on the thoroughfare.

The discovery which followed was still more perplexing. Directly beneath the hole at the apex of the hollow was positioned a large, flat stone – faintly engraved with a spiralling triskelion. The protocol of recording its precise position in the burial complex was tacitly abandoned, as the anthropologists rapidly worked to remove it from the clay. It was devilishly heavy, but by now there was enough room in the chamber for both men to stand, and, with Dr. Hugog's sinews straining like the strings of an orchestral violin; his bones like its bow – heave it away. It was not, as both men had assumed, a grave-marker. No remains, no sacred skulls lay crushed beneath. Instead there gaped the dumb and pitchy void of another hole. 'What on earth – what sort of a passage tomb is this?' whispered the doctor. 'Perhaps this chamber is simply a glorified lobby', murmured Casimir, 'an elaborate propylaea to some sacral necropolis far below'. Dr. Hugog lowered the lantern down as far as his long arm could stretch. 'I can't see anything… let's try and plumb it'. Casimir produced a half-spent ball of twine which he typically used to measure the area and gradient of shallow digs. Fixing a stone weight to its end, they let it fall – watching the whole thing unravel before reaching the bottom of the hole. The string swayed faintly, as if in a breeze. The chamber was silent. Without speaking, Dr. Hugog picked up a flint and dropped it down. After a minute, the chamber was still silent. Two minutes. 'It must have gotten embedded in the walls of the shaft' muttered the doctor. 'Or perhaps it's just bottomless', whispered Casimir, 'perhaps it really leads… somewhere beyond'.  Dr. Hugog said nothing. Though he would never admit it to the other man, this portal in the ground – large enough for a man, and apparently moulded, like the entrance-ways, from the calcareous rock itself – was the locus of the barrow's magnetism. It was the plughole in the bathtub of the cosmos, and the nearer he came, the more forcefully he felt its vortex swirl.

It was hard to focus on the rest of the excavation. Using some planks that had served as supports before the tunnel collapse, they covered up the hole in the ground – partially to stop themselves stumbling in, and partially, Dr. Hugog thought, to temporarily avoid any further confrontation with the troubling fact of its existence. The far side of the chamber was still piled with the centuries' accumulation of detritus. They paused for their customary teatime on the surface, and Dr. Hugog stretched his knobbled spine for the first time in what felt like hours, audibly producing the sound of a badly tuned xylophone. And then they descended once more. Ask any soul in full possession of their wits, and they would tell you that no surprise more deranging than the bottomless pit already uncovered could await within the inner sanctum of Gogoth's Tump. They would (unless, of course, you had been shrewd enough to ask a fellow of the Society for Amateur Anthropologists), invariably answer in the negative – and they would also invariably be mistaken. Again I shall spare you the details of its gradual discovery, the painstaking removal of layers of dirt, the suspension of lanterns to work unimpeded, the mounting fervour of the men as they slowly comprehended the magnitude of what they had discovered. The nature of their find, however, I shall reveal in full. For on the far wall of the inner chamber, now fully cleared of debris, Dr. Hugog and Owain Casimir were staring dumbfounded at a complete *mural*, a rupestrian *epic* of palaeolithic artistry and imagination.

The templates of hands were so numerous that they overlapped, distorted like the erosive moorings of limpets on some ancestral shore. Their long and equivalent fingers wove a border about the scene, like russet grasses waving in the lanternlight. But what predominated was the depiction of the *monster*. It was a giant, gaunt and strange, like an evening shadow in red ochre. It was shaggy with lines that stuck out from its body at every angle. Its claws were long and glyptic. Its brutish face bulged with eyes of negative space, a carnivorous mess of dots and jags below. And as Dr. Hugog looked on, he saw that the beast wasn't alone – in fact, it was portrayed *twice*. The first scene was highly disturbing. It portrayed the giant crowded by feminine figures, gravid as crude idols of fertility, lavishing it with perverse adoration. Further down the wall, these same blobby mothers were presented in greater size and resolution, and from their loins there appeared to be spilling a great army; a whole race of twisted men. These men were tall and lean as nomads, carrying weapons wrought from arc and line – and each one was detailed, with the precise detail of a frayed-twig brush, with a crown of claws upon their iconographic hands. The second scene plainly showed the monster as victim of a hunt. A cohort of much smaller figures, elegant in their primitivism, were hurling lines and dots at its great body, curving with cowardice. A third scene followed. The little men, victorious in their primitive gigantomachy, had turned their attention upon the monster's hybrid spawn. Despite their smaller size, they appeared far more numerous and co-ordinated, and iron pigment approached haemoglobin. Another section showed lots of the little men carrying what at first looked like arrows, but on closer inspection more likely signified sheaves of grain, from little circles in the ground towards a much larger circle rimmed with concentric dots. There were three prominent circles of charcoal in its centre – and above it hung a rough cruciform, each arm a sheaf of wheat. 'St. Brigid's cross?' breathed Dr. Hugog in disbelief, 'but – that's so *late*... all this can't have originated in the fifth century – it's preposterous!' His heart was pounding, and his head ached as if in prelude to some thunderous cranial birth. Owain Casimir looked on at the painting, hypnotised. Smaller cruciforms were scattered around the besieging ranks of the third scene – as if to identify the allegiance of the little men, whose diminutive size precluded characterising details. 'Preposterous, no – certainly unusual, certainly atavistic... but even if it is a fifth century creation, who's to say *when* all this was supposed to have occurred?' 'When? It's *mythology*, Casimir-', began Dr. Hugog in frenzy, and stopped when his eyes rested on the mural's final scene. The largest ring appeared again, filled with those same dot-stick assemblages representing wheat or barley; the three circles gaping at its nucleus, the cereal cruciform hovering above. It was Gogoth's Tump – it had to be! And all around, on top and inside it, little men were leading larger men, long-fingered women and their goblin children, corralling them with sharp lines and flung blotches – until their lean bodies, reduced to rigid sticks, were indistinguishable from the linework of the scattered grain. The dark circles in the centre of it all sucked at them like hungry mouths.

'This is the find of the century' whispered Casimir amidst the reverie – 'the find of the century!' He clasped Dr. Hugog's hand and started laughing with glee. 'Why so stricken, doctor? This is remarkable! Unlike anything I've ever seen – I dare say, unlike anything you've ever seen! I have to show my grandfather – Dr. Hugog, thank you. Thank you, thank you!' And without a moment's pause, the younger man scampered through the portal and into the evening air. Dr. Hugog was motionless. The dusk had grown cloudy, and no light funnelled through the vertical shaft. Bathed in lanternlight, the doctor collapsed onto the planks over the hole in the floor. He could not peel his eyes away from the mural – so savage, so haunting, so recent – and so *real*. He had not found the birthplace of the Cult of the Skull – but he had learned something of still greater importance and profundity. His brain throbbed madly in his head. What he was looking at – what was sketched in lurid charcoal and crimson on the grimy chalk of the inner dome – was the record of an ancient genocide. This isolated place had to be, until recent centuries, the refugium of a hominin species evolutionarily anterior to man. These people, hunter-gatherers, were ritually annihilated by the superior organisation of early agrarians – the Druid's 'good Christian folks', no doubt – who took them for the pagan spawn of giants. Apart from the grotesque gigantomachy, the wall-art did not present a single hunting scene, which meant that it had to have been created by the sedentary, agricultural victors. Dr. Hugog shivered. Yet he knew that their appalling massacres had not been entirely victorious. This realisation was bound up with another – that the 'glandular condition' from which he had suffered since birth could be no such thing. For it was the same monstrous height, strange hands, and wanderlust that belonged to these people which haunted his own genetic material. And Dr. Hugog had always pondered the unknown significance of his local, Irish roots.

\*\*\*

That evening the doctor could think of nothing but returning to the barrow. Alzada and Henry could wait, as they had waited, with his love and good wishes for company – for he had had uncovered the tomb of his ancestors, his ur-family, and it was an urgent, inner imperative to find them. There was only one place they could be – somewhere in the cavernous void beneath Gogoth's Tump. What unexplored labyrinths, what undelved underworlds of prehistoric mystery awaited him there? Dr. Hugog could not even begin to speculate. But that dark opening called to him, pulled him ever closer, ever further into that ancient past still alive in his blood, in his bones, in the stratigraphic cores of each and every cell – and he was beginning to feel himself slip. That night he prepared a length of rope he had found in his hovel, and stayed up fashioning crampons from a pair of bent old horseshoes and the rusty heads of gardening tools. He had earned some caving experience in Spain. There it had helped him find a magnificently preserved object of Skull Cult worship – and here it would serve a still nobler cause.

He left early the following morning, earlier than he and Mr. Casimir usually met at the farmhouse to discuss plans for the day's excavation before making the walk to Gogoth's Tump. He picked a shrivelled apple from a low bough, which the frost had nearly blackened – and slowly ate it on the way, leaning hard on his stick to support the weight of his new equipment. The mound rose into view, denuded of its guardian oak, and half-ravaged by the forces of anthropological advance. In the grey light of morning, it was an almost pensive sight, but Dr. Hugog did not let a contemplative attitude divert his purpose. Leaving his stick by the tunnel's mouth, he inclined his stately back and entered, shrinking further into himself with every step, like the hidden body of a snail folding up and away into the topmost crannies of its shell. Soon he had squeezed through the portal, and was inside the chalky dome of the inner sanctum. A jury of gaunt, organic figures scrutinised his ignition of the lantern-light; the beastly judges snarled in mummified contempt. He attached his rope to the sturdiest tunnel support, allowing himself just over twenty meters with which to descend. His hope was to find a lateral chamber: the vertical shafts of pyramids, he knew, were often rich in such structures. He removed the wooden planks and stared down into the black and whirling infinite. He could hear *voices* – faint, distant voices, singing like birds, calling in a guttural tongue unheard for millennia. He thought of the beautiful Alzada, and dear young Henry's pure clairvoyant mind. He yearned to see them again, he truly did – but nobody, *nobody* could blame him for this…

The rock fell with plutonic force. Dr. Hugog did not even have time to shape the phrase 'lithobolia' in his brain before the sustaining fluids of that miraculous organ were mixing with the cold clay of the chamber ground. Owain Casimir entered the chamber, and admired his work. The angle from the upper shaft to the doctor's head could not have been more perfect. He helped his grandfather in through the portal. Both were dressed in the white chasubles of their order, marked with the golden sigil of St. Brigid's cross, a human skull leering at its base. Casimir pulled Dr. Hugog's legs from the hole, laid his body out and stripped it naked, while the Druid haphazardly scattered golden wheat from a bushel they had picked at the farmhouse. Now the ritual could begin. Casimir tilted a gourd-like vessel to his grandfather's lips. The old man moved like a somnambulist, animated only by the dim mnemonics of childhood recollection – and while his grandson held the doctor's limp hand against the wall, the Druid released a mist of red pigment from his cheeks. A new trophy glistened in the mound, glistened redly as the sanguine ichor bedewing the old man's whiskers. Owain bent to kiss his grandfather, holding him in a prolonged embrace, transferring the colour to his own face and robe. The sound of the Druid's prayers, muttered in the old tongue, echoed off the domed walls as the younger man seized Hugog by the shoulders and dragged his frail corpse to the pit. 'Spawn of Gogoth, spawn of Gog, father of giants, we return your child to the underworld. Curses break his heathen head'. The doctor's body tumbled gracelessly into the abyss, and where, or *whether*, it ever came to rest – neither celebrant could rightly say. The Casimirs pulled the great stone back over the hole, where it fitted neatly, and once more embraced.

The young man slowly lifted his grandfather's hat from his head. He guided the Druid down, helping him sit on the stone above the pit. Standing beside him, he could see the bald crown of his cranium – it was dented and cratered with the concavities of a hundred ritual trepanations. His perforated braincase was open to the universe. Casimir took his own hat off, and felt a strange tingle in the squishy patch that marked his own trepanation. One day, he knew, he would see as clearly as the Druid. Sunlight crawled like time over their skin, excavating wrinkles by the addition of shadow. He knew it fell also on the cross of St. Brigid that now stood atop the mound, taking the place of the oak from whose bones it had been fashioned.

'What do you see, Grandfather?' croaked Owain. The Druid closed his eyes – and opened them. He gazed out from the terrible vacant socket of Gogoth, through which the men had entered to sit precisely where his monstrous brainstem had once connected to his spine. Such power had been native to the enemy kind. Sunlight spilled through the trepanation in the giant's fossilised skull, filling the hollow, painted dome of his braincase with celestial radiance. Great Gogoth, father of evil. Great Gogoth, the ancient adversary, slain long ago by the founders of their order, the Cult of the Skull, to cleanse the world of heathenry. Great and terrible, the mighty Gogoth – who had been the doctor's earliest ancestor, and who had lived on within him.

'He has a son', whispered the Druid, and Casimir's hand clasped the letter in his pocket.

# EREMIEL

The circumstances of my elevation to the high table of the London Mythophysical Society were, in a characteristic trick of destiny, the precise circumstances of my subsequent exclusion and present state of hiding. Right now I am sitting at a very low table – the table of a disreputable chophouse, chain-smoking the weak tobacco which makes up the bulk of my earthly possessions, and chain-drinking even weaker coffee. I am trying to write. I doubt I shall be able to evade the attentions of the Society for much longer, and dread to think what might come of me when they finally catch up – but for now I must make certain that the truth of those wretched circumstances is put to paper, as bizarre and fantastical as they might at first appear.

If I can thank my current extremity for one thing it is the swift and unflinching annulment of that existential tedium which has heretofore characterised my existence. Since my earliest recollection, life has principally consisted of a sort of arbitrary dynamic equilibrium: things go up, then things go down, then up again, and so on forever, pumping the handcart into hell. I have met no-one else who can walk from one side of town to the other with both direction and purpose and still end up precisely where they started, which in my case invariably turned out to be the East End dockyards, and specifically Lady Mei's. There I would light the opium-lamp and extinguish it again. I would inhale the slumbrous fumes and exhale them again. I would enjoy a brief respite from drudgery, counting curlicues of vapour and finding poetry in the patterns of the squalid rugs – before returning again, and again, and again. At this time I had for some months been ankle-deep in the apathetic hunt for a lodgings, and was slowly coming to think – what with the proportion of nights I spent dithering in Lady Mei's opulent nowhere – that it would be better not to deceive myself with false desires to escape this particular purgatory. Many people, I am told, experience life as a sort of rhythm. For me it is merely a bodyless whine, as from a great mosquito. The effect of these incessant acclivities and declivities of the psyche *in toto* might be expressed as the reduction of essentially stable experience to the shimmering oscillations of a high-frequency mirage. A fool's stability, to be found in endless shifting – but it was the only one I had. In consequence, and in spite of my habitual malingering amongst merchantmen and sailors, I had never quite developed the sea-legs for my own mortal vessel, and so was in grave danger of remaining forever tossed up and down, up and down on the ocean of everyday existence.

That was until my encounter with a stranger on the docks. It was very early on a Friday morning, I seem to recall, so early that the sun was still soaked in an albumen capsule of cloud; bald of that fiery plumage that daily grows to burn off the cold river mist. I had crawled out of Lady Mei's after a particularly soporific sojourn, quite uncertain of the time or the place – only sure of the craving for cool air, and desirous of watching the bustle of the docks through parting veils of dream. Shipments were already beginning to pour in. Longshoremen extricated themselves from the woodwork, shivering in that same morning cold which I welcomed with relish after a night of greasy oil-lamps and the recumbent sprawl of sweating bodies. My stranger, evidently, did not share this affection. A sturdy-looking gentleman of uncertain extraction had clasped my shoulder, shaking me from the reverie which was really just another manifestation of my existential torpor. "Ere', he said, pressing a guinea into my hand with a scrap of paper, 'you pick up the shipment for Dr. Amari and fetch it to 'im. I can't take these bloody mornins' anymore', he shivered, and stumbled into Lady Mei's. I very nearly stumbled in after him. Perhaps the gentleman had mistaken me for some sort of harbourmaster – I was, after all, dressed in my customary rumpled pinstripe and stolen waistcoat – or perhaps he simply thought he was doing some layabout a favour. Either way, the stranger could not have known how much I detested responsibility of any kind, nor guessed at how this spontaneous employment had entrusted me with so much more of it than the lollygagging in which I had fully intended to squander my morning. And yet I also knew that to enter the opium den at this hour, guinea in hand, would not see me out again for a very long time indeed. I considered my options. The dockland air was refreshing and cool, a melange of tar and hemp and that peculiar smell, common to rivers, which can only be described as the angel's share of mud. Pheromones enough for the courtship of a whim. And so I read the stranger's crumpled letter of instruction, and began to range the docks in search of Dr. Amari's mysterious shipment.

The *Fenghuang* was already half-unloaded in its berth when I threaded my way through the ruck of stevedores standing on the stones, waving my letter of instruction. A swarthy fellow at the gangs snatched the docket and looked me up and down, as if he expected someone altogether different. But though my dissolute appearance must have made the man suspicious of underhand business, this same suggestion of moral atrophy correlated mercifully with a muscular variety whose progression would almost certainly have thwarted the execution of any crooked dealings. He handed back the letter with a grunt, before barking unintelligently into the hold. For a dreadful moment I wondered as to the nature of this shipment – whether I had been enlisted to shiver my spine hauling a half-tonne crate around town – and then, for a slightly more alluring one, whether Dr. Amari's consignment might perhaps be of pecuniary value. I imagined far-fetched rarities, Orient silks and island wines. If indeed this was the case, I swiftly resolved to send the good doctor (whose address was on the letter) a detailed note explicating their tragic loss overboard. But surely, even a stranger seized by the most wanton caprice would not have entrusted a rogue like myself with such a burden. Of course, when the loader-boy emerged from the hold, I knew that my speculations had been in vain. Things go up – things come down.

The shipment was neither particularly awkward nor, apparently, worth stealing. It was a densely woven gunny-sack, about the displacement of a nine-month babe, and not at all as heavy. It smelled extremely fragrant. Its contents jingled slightly in my arms. It was printed with the single word *CEYLON*. It was probably full of untreated spices, I thought, of the kind sought after by bootleg perfumers or still more wretched criminals like the candlemakers' guild – but emphatically not by gentlemen thieves. And so I slung the bag over my shoulder, nodded a cursory 'thanks' to the deckhand, and consulted my letter of instruction, determined to deliver Dr. Amari's slightly underwhelming shipment as commissioned.

The address, in truth, was not what I had been expecting. A few streets away from the docks and the rabble stood a rather derelict boarding-house, three stories tall, with just enough portico, perron and pilaster intact to bequeath an air of undead splendour. A tar-painted sign creaked over the gate, simply reading 'rooms'. I went inside, suddenly awash with a curiously inverted vertigo as the ceiling fell away overhead. It was so incongruously high and elegant that the egg-and-dart ornamentation of its crown moulding appeared sculpted solely for the private contemplation of the athanatoi. The same could not be said for the rest of the ground floor, however, or at least the foyer in which I presently stood. In fact, the lofty ceilings were the only aspect of the edifice which did not appear subject to what I could only speculate was a near-constant project of renovation – and only because nobody could reach them. A scratch in the wall revealed strata of wallpaper dense as a deck of cards. A missing tile revealed another pattern beneath, probably all the way down, I imagined, to Roman mosaic. The furniture ran the gamut from venerable antiquity to the latest modern style, with vague intimations of the fact that one was slowly being outphased by the other, with the direction of exchange being anybody's guess. The scene was tied together by a centrepiece rug which, on the evidence of its pristine condition, must have been placed there minutes before I arrived. I asked the landlady if she might inform me whether one Dr. Amari was in residence, and if so, where might I find his apartments. She looked me up and down, eyes fixing on the bag I was carrying, as though she rather expected somebody else. This was beginning to vex me slightly, but before I could vocalise my displeasure, she shrugged her shoulders. 'Omar never did like the cold', she said, 'but I reckon you'll do just fine. And Dr. Amari is always in residence, mister. He *is* one hundred and thirty-five years old'.

The landlady offered to take me up to his rooms. 'One hundred and thirty-five years old?' I asked, following her up the creaking stairs. 'Yes', she said simply, and knocked politely on a heavy old door. We were on the uppermost level of the shabby and unorthodox rooming establishment, and it suddenly occurred to me that some of the chambers we had passed might indeed be vacant and, to judge by their décor, attainable for one of my limited means. I resolved to enquire on this point once my errand was completed – but before I could muse further on the particularities of spaciousness and style, a thin voice wafted from beyond the door. 'Come in'.

The landlady opened it with some effort. The heady aroma of spice whorled out of the chambers with the force of a poltergeist. 'Thank you, Mrs. Waldrop' came the same frail voice, to which the landlady nodded genially before descending the uneven stair, leaving me to flounder in a riptide of fragrance. 'Come in, young man, come in' croaked Dr. Amari – and I did, for once, exactly as I was told. The room was gigantic. I suspect a wall had been knocked down to achieve such an effect, which was perfectly in character for a house like this. An antechamber was separated by drapes of heavy brocade, ornamented with designs like the tailfeathers of peacocks in flower. An articulated writing desk, stacked bookshelves and reading-wheel dominated the far side of the room, and in its centre, beneath a great arch-topped window (which I swear I had not observed from outside) was a great claw-footed four-poster, tasselled drapes of burgundy girded about each pillar like ceremonial robes. Beside was situated a lacquered teapoy, on which a beautiful teapot shone like a crystal ball. Nearby, like the shed exoskeleton of some arabesque crustacean, stood the frame of an antique wheeled chair, a bronze chariot with a team of two miniature penny-farthings. All things of great age and value. And reclining on the bed beneath coverlets of silk, was Dr. Amari himself.

One hundred and thirty-five years struck me as a conservative estimate for the fellow's age. His skin was like papyrus into which the years had etched hieroglyphs of ruin. His hands, steepled over the spread, were like twisted branches, and each finger was tipped with a long translucent talon. Most curious however was his… *apparatus*. Visible through satin robes, his frail chest was encased in what I can only describe as a mechanised sleeve; small motors whirring in rhythmical contractions, a spinal cord of pipes and wires trailing away from the device and into the curtained room. A small bellows, powered by the same mechanisms, fed air through a tube into the doctor's nose, which was covered by a nosepiece ornate as the bulb of a gilded aspergillum. It made his voice sound thin and nasal. His head was supported by a throne of pillows, and he wore a crystal eyeglass that flashed when he spoke. 'It appears that mister Omar finally grew weary of the morning cold. But do come in, I said, young man, come in! Do not be alarmed, if that is indeed alarm I detect, and not reverence'.

I took another step towards the bed. 'Dr. Amari, I presume? I've brought your shipment'. 'Exquisite', wheezed the reclining figure, and patted the bed with a shrunken claw. I walked forward and gave him the bag, which he hungrily slashed open with his thumbnail. Brown scrolls of bark spilled out in a pungent cloud, dusting the silks with fine ochre. My nostrils had grown accustomed to the powerful odour of the place, but this action fully renewed their sensitivity. 'The finest Ceylon *Cinnamomum*' mused the ancient gentleman, 'finely delivered' – and as he spoke, I realised that cinnamon was indeed the apartment's dominant note. 'Here boy'. Dr. Amari reached beneath his mound of pillows, extracting another guinea, 'and the same again next Friday if you will. Can I offer you some tea?' He leaned over to the crystal teapot, handsome as an imperial urn, and poured himself a cup. The porcelain was so fine that the tea cast a shadow straight through it.

I bowed to collect the guinea, catching another concentrated whiff of cinnamon from the teapot. It was only with the offer of spiced tea that I realised how unbearably hot the doctor's chambers were. I removed my jacket, revealing an amphibian underbelly of pilfered waistcoat and distained evening shirt. There wasn't even a fire in the hearth. 'A kind offer, doctor, which I shall have to decline,' I said with consummate charm, unfolding the letter of instruction from my pocket, 'but I shall be seeing you again next Friday?' 'To be certain', he said, 'there is always a necessity for cinnamon. Well met, young fellow', he said, his thin voice further diluted by the rhythmical gyrations of his apparatus. The bellows rose and fell like the ribcage of a dreaming child; up and down, I thought, so perpetually up and down that they might as well not be moving at all. As I turned to leave, Dr. Amari picked up a book from the pile at his bedside – and I stopped myself. 'Doctor', I began cautiously, 'is it true that you are – forgive me – one hundred and thirty-five years of age?' 'No', he said from behind his book, 'one hundred and thirty-eight'. His eyepiece flashed with inscrutable mirth as we made our farewells, and I made off with a silver teaspoon, its handle inlaid with mother-of-pearl.

The chambers below Dr. Amari were entirely unoccupied. 'People have complained about the smell,' warned Mrs. Waldrop, as I made my deposit with a wad of notes in trust, a few dubious cheques and a handful of guineas, 'of Dr. Amari's cinnamon. You can nose it all hours of the night and day. Some say it gets… sickly'. That didn't worry me too much.

In fact, the fragrance differed only by a factor of intensity from that which I customarily inhaled amongst the Malay spicers in the slump at Lady Mei's. The room was very reasonably priced, and had a ceiling like a philosopher's forehead. I found myself thanking the dockyard stranger for this stroke of serendipity – and serendipity it certainly was, for the cinnamon I had been employed to deliver hailed from Serendip itself, from fair and finely-scented Ceylon. Now I could loiter about the docks with no pretensions of purpose – no vague feeling that I should have to pick myself up off the rug and search for a boarding-house later in the day. I could drift merrily between those upstrokes and downswings that structured my meaningless existence.

But there was one thing that troubled my idealisations – and that was the enigma of Dr. Amari. Mrs. Waldrop told me he had already been firmly embedded in the boarding-house when she took over as landlady nearly two decades ago – but that he paid his fees unfailingly, and she held no compunction against reliable commerce. He had been part of the family business for so long that she almost considered him part of the family – indeed, for this reason, and because she knew how much he enjoyed conversation, Mrs. Waldrop took care to bring Dr. Amari two full meals a day at no cost whatsoever. The ancient doctor was entirely confined to his chambers and his apparatus – but his presence was known throughout the building by the pervasive smell of cinnamon. Come to think of it, for what reason might such a man require so regular a shipment of the stuff? No-one could get through so much spiced tea in a week. And while Dr. Amari was no rogue perfumer (that much alone was certain), might it perhaps have something to do with his evidently lavish wealth? Whether or not he really was a hundred and thirty-something (which was, incidentally, impossible), how indeed could such an ancient afford to rent, stock, and renovate an entire apartment for twenty years and more without ever leaving it? It was a secret my empty pockets might dearly benefit from knowing. And so I resolved to strike up a rapport with my mysterious employer when next I bore his shipment from the docks.

Despite my recent acquisition of a hospitable chamber, I still found myself, like a lonely shepherdess, dreaming my evenings away at the pipe. Sometimes I was able to collect some meagre royalties from the printer's office. While my premature rustication from the Cathedral School (for the grave error, might I add, of 'persistent and excessive hypnogogia') had rather interrupted my literary aspirations, I had still managed to harvest enough wit and wisdom there to fuel occasional ramblings for the less savoury London periodicals.

These would sporadically worm their way into publication, and sprinkle my purse with poppyseed – indeed, I found a great tranquillity in focusing the endless oscillations of my life into those of a penpoint. But my thoughts kept returning to the strange old cyborg in the apartment overhead, and it was with considerable curiosity and hobnail tap-tapping on the quayside that I found myself awaiting Dr. Amari's cinnamon – and making sure it arrived precisely as requested.

Opening the doctor's door was like standing before the hellmouth of a baker's oven, heat and spice whomped into me like a wall. 'Come in, young man, come in, come in!' I saluted my wizened host, passed him the cinnamon, and received my guinea. Apart from a few stray quills on the floor, I noticed that last week's shipment was nowhere in evidence. The bellows at Dr. Amari's breast looked fine enough to be woven out of batwing, almost flapping as the apparatus massaged the old man's thorax like a wraparound heart. Very soon each pulse of its eternal rhythm blended with the silence dividing it from the next, so that my brain received nothing but a protracted monotone, just as the throbbing of my own heart faded into the whistle of blood against eardrum in the opium-trance. 'That is a most ingenious machine', I proffered. 'My thanks', said Dr. Amari – 'I'd be seen dead without it.' His laugh was like a genie coughing through a canyon, or a draught hissing through an abandoned leprosarium. 'Can I offer you some tea?', he continued, 'and do you have a name?' I accepted his offer, and gave him one. 'Very good', he said with a sly grin, pouring the rich cinnamon infusion with a slight tremor of his claws. 'I must say, I am extremely grateful for your services. The spice is invaluable… for my studies'.

I paused to take off my jacket in the sweltering apartment. There was nowhere to sit, so I perched on the floor. 'I take it you are a man of learning, doctor?' The recumbent figure drew a long breath through his nosepiece. 'Defrocked', he enunciated with fallen grandeur, 'and beleaguered'. Like the engraving of an actor unto an audience of ghosts, he raised a hand towards the teetering bookshelves. For one of such profound eld, I thought, the man's wits were uncommonly agile. 'When I first came to this city, I was told that my studies would be far too *esoteric* for pursuit in the Cathedral academies – and so they proved. It was a great fortune, therefore' – Dr. Amari waited for his apparatus to shore up the widening gulf between his matter and his mind – 'to find my tenure with the London Mythophysical Society'.

I had never heard of it. But if Dr. Amari was tenured, then perhaps it could explain his wealth. 'And the nature of your studies?' I asked, taking a tentative sip of the tea now that it was cooler, and resolving not to take another on account of the overwhelming taste of cinnamon. Machinery whirred. 'I am writing a book', he resumed, 'for the Society. *The Book of Eremiel*. That is the present focus of my research'. Sure enough, the writing-desk was piled with the autumn leaves of a dismembered manuscript. There was a fire in his eyeglass that bespoke the unique enthusiasm of the nascent lecturer, and I received the distinct impression that Mrs. Waldrop's conversation, while surely pleasant, never lit upon the theme of the doctor's studies.

I was just about to pursue my questioning – how indeed, I wanted to know, was this *Book of Eremiel* connected with cinnamon? – when that same affable woman pushed open the door with a tray of breakfast and a fresh teapot. 'You'll excuse me, doctor', she said, wading into our convocation, 'but I raided your larder for the eggs when I came in this morning'. 'Not to worry' wheezed the old man, hauling himself aright with the crackling of mummified shoulders, 'I am ever grateful for your care, Mrs. Waldrop. Young man, let us suspend our colloquy. Bring more cinnamon next Friday, yes? Very good'. I stood up from the floor, wiping the sweat from my brow. 'I ought to mention, Dr. Amari – I have taken a room downstairs'. The eyeglass twinkled. 'Well, come up for tea again soon then! But anon – anon. I must unto my banquet – and my rest'. The exertion of talking had taken its toll on the doctor. As I headed downstairs I could hear him inhale juddering breaths from his bellows, even over the cricket-chorus of his whispering device. I drank the cool and unspiced air like spring water; my skull vibrating with speculations. The doctor was a fascinating character – and perhaps a valuable asset. I had covertly returned the silver teaspoon; slipping it out of my pocket and leaving it with my saucer.

Over the following week I suspect I visited Dr. Amari's apartments about as often as I visited Lady Mei's. Indeed, I found that our discourse had a similarly narcotic effect. For starters, it appeared to disobey the laws of time – or at the very least to quibble with their footnotes. It also possessed the admirable and addictive quality of opening a brief window into transcendent comprehension, before closing it in such a manner as to make it impossible to recall what exactly you thought you had understood. In other words, ups soared and downs plummeted. I was mostly interested in his work – and in the nature of the London Mythophysical Society, that occulted coalition of learned souls committed to 'finding old answers to new questions'.

'How might one come to write for such a Society?' I remember asking, 'and more importantly, how might one go about acquiring membership?' Dr.

Amari told me that it would be wise not to bother myself with such questions – it was extraordinarily exclusive, you see, and to even be considered for a space on the high table, one had to submit the answer to an immemorial mystery, and upon review, one's answer had to be found *correct*. Yet he had also let slip the incredibly lucrative nature of this achievement. Some elevated people, I gathered, were willing to pay extraordinary amounts of money to see old secrets unravelled – the same sorts of people, I imagined, who would pay a month's wages to see charlatans crowbarring canopic jars in disused operating theatres. Even an article for the Society's subterraneously circulated journal – released once a year from the jaws of some obscure private press – would be worth a small fortune, if accepted. And although he never said so outright, I found myself suspecting that, throughout the last century of his life, Dr. Amari had been a rather prolific contributor.

I wish I could transcribe more of what I still remember of our teatime convocations, but I am running out of groats to pay for this horrible coffee, and dread to stay too long in one place. Nonetheless I shall relate as much as I can. Dr. Amari tended towards reticence on the topic of *The Book of Eremiel*, and what little he chanced to reveal seemed almost extravagantly disconnected from everything else that it allegedly treated. 'What's the new question?' I one day happened to ask. Dr. Amari looked bemused. 'I beg your pardon?' 'If the London Mythophysical Society seeks old answers to new questions, doctor – I can only assume that *The Book of Eremiel* is directed towards unravelling some modern quandary?' Dr. Amari swivelled to face me. For this encounter I had chanced to catch the old man at his articulated writing desk, sitting in his strange wheeled chair with a braid of pipes and cords trailing off into the antechamber. 'Very astute of you, young man – and quite so. This I shall tell you. Several years ago, it came to my attention that a gentleman of the Cathedral School had stumbled upon a very large question indeed – perhaps, it might fairly be stated, the largest one of all – the question concerning the origins of our universe'.

Our conversations had a curious cadence. Every so often the doctor would fall mute while the motors of his apparatus chugged hard to revivify his frail faculties. During these silences it became customary for me to hold my tongue – partially out of deference to the noise of the machine, and partially because I came to suspect that, when such lulls occurred, the doctor was incapable of experiencing anything at all. But he always returned, and so continued our dialogue. 'To this question he proposed a solution – a solution which has come to be known as the Ekpyrotic Model. How good is your etymology, boy?' 'Notoriously imprecise'. 'Very good. It comes from the Greek *ekpyrōsis*, meaning 'conflagration' – or more specifically, through the prefix 'ek', meaning *from* the conflagration. He proposes that the universe is without true beginning, and that it is instead trapped' – another mechanical interruption, followed by a long draught of spiced tea – 'in an endless cycle of rebirth and dissolution'. 'How interesting'. 'Indeed – though the calculations by which he seeks to prove such a fancy are, well, to put it in the vernacular, utter bunkum. One cannot hope to successfully theorise what is effectively a cosmic machine for perpetual motion without violating some of the fundamental strictures upon which it is founded. This is not to say, however, that the concept is without merit. On the contrary – I simply feel that it requires an older answer. The Stoics intimated as such, as did the Hindus, with their Kalpa. But no-one has quite brought it to fruition' – I waited patiently as again the apparatus droned – 'yet'. And on the subject he would say no more.

Another time I asked the doctor about 'Eremiel'. This too elicited a particularly curious response. 'I can tell you freely what Eremiel *was*, young man – but nobody must know what Eremiel *is*'. The doctor had a weakness for such arcane formulations, and I could tell they amused him greatly. 'Do go on', I pleaded, pouring another cup of cinnamon tea; a gesture which had increasingly become my privilege, so as not to exhaust my interlocutor. I couldn't risk the curtailment of these conversations for so trivial a thing as physical necessity. 'If you wish', he eventually said with a glint of his eyeglass. 'Eremiel, you see, was an archangel – mentioned variously throughout apocrypha, and in several of the deuterocanonical testaments, I believe. He is a figure of tremendous interest – and enormous value – to me and my work'. 'Oh yes?' I prompted. 'Yes indeed'. 'And why… might this be?' 'Young man, you ask many questions. But this much I shall tell you. In some sources, Eremiel guards the gates of heaven alongside St. Peter. In others, Eremiel is the angel of destruction. And in still others…' I waited for the apparatus to do its work, 'Eremiel presides over Sheol, the middle space, spanning life and death. He is depicted with a set of scales. Sometimes they are in balance. Sometimes one side is up, and sometimes the other. And sometimes… both sides are up, and both sides are down'. I paused to consider. 'I must confess to you, doctor – that image rather tents to the quick. By which I mean only to say, you happen to have chanced upon a rather fitting metaphor for my own life. I think I have spoken to you before about the arbitrary dynamic equilibrium of things'. 'Indeed', said Dr. Amari, 'mine too – dare I say more fitting than most. But remember, boy –

this is emphatically *not* what Eremiel *is*'. And on this subject also, I could extract nothing more.

There were, in truth, only three unbreakable taboos delimiting our discussion. The first concerned the contents of the curtained antechamber, into which snaked the various nerves and arteries of what was now obviously Dr. Amari's life-supporting apparatus. The only harsh word I had ever received from the old doctor was his response to whether I might go inside and look. The second taboo involved overmuch prying at certain texts, and especially the unfinished *Book of Eremiel*, which was often visible on the writing desk, though never close enough to read. And the third – which irritated me increasingly, and far more than the other two – concerned the precise nature and purpose of the cinnamon which I was weekly employed to deliver. I accepted my payment without complaint, which had now, with a touch of persuasion, increased to two guineas – but the rent for my chamber was approaching soon, and my debt at Lady Mei's had increased to the point that I would avoid visiting on nights that I knew the proprietess herself would be present. People said that her ivory hairpin was the sheath of a poisoned needle – deployed more liberally than one might think. But it began to irk me deeply that the same raw spice which earned me two guineas a week would doubtless earn Dr. Amari –

through what mysterious research I could not even begin to conjecture – hundreds of pounds. I had thought by now, with nearly a month of boiling, cinnamon-scented teatimes under my belt, however edifying they otherwise proved, to have extracted the secret and even perhaps made something of an industry of it. I had thought it possible to ride the 'up' long enough to outpace the 'down' – but it was becoming very clear that, as usual, I had simply been coasting along the millpond of middle space. The doctor was undeniably a fascinating character – but I would need to work harder – and more swiftly – if he was to become a valuable asset.

The same day I had first shaped coherent thought from my discontent, I pressed Dr. Amari to tell me about the cinnamon. Why so much of it – what did he use it for – and what did it mean? He flatly refused to tell me. After a few more attempts the old man excused himself, citing exhaustion – but I knew his craft. For all his years, he had not fallen into senility – on the contrary, he seemed to have fallen upwards into ever more dazzling heights of intellect – and so I took this slippery refusal, however warranted it might have been, as nothing less than a betrayal of trust. All the time I spent hovering at Dr. Amari's bedside in luxuriant discourse had robbed me of time to spend on my own writing, and by now the trickle of royalties from the printer's office had entirely dried up. The situation grew increasingly dire. I could not risk eviction from the rooming-house (whose foyer had, incidentally, been redecorated at least twice during my occupancy), or I would lose contact with a man who held the secret to seemingly infinite wealth – and I could certainly not risk banishment from Lady Mei's, lest my brain short-circuit for want of dream. I resolved to resort to most desperate measures.

It was under the cloak of a foul and smog-choked night that I slunk down to the dockyards and into the rancid swelter of the opium-den. It was raining thick as frogspawn, with puddles like smeared petroleum glistening on the wharf. Guineas jingled at my hip – but I was not here to chase the customary dragon. When at last I emerged, my pockets had lightened greatly, despite multiplying in fullness – and how Dr. Amari would have enjoyed that formulation, I thought bitterly, as I made my way back through pattering globules of storm. A single electric lantern flickered in my room (Mrs. Waldrop did not mind the lights burning late so long as they were inadequate) and in its yellow radiance I unloaded a cargo to rival Dr. Amari's cinnamon. Two dry fistfuls of poppyheads, rattling with unborn dreams like dice in a cup. Slowly, methodically, I shook out their seeds on the table, wasting nothing but the husks which I crushed and threw away like trepanated skulls. I pulverised them with the heel of my hobnail, turning the seeds into fine powder – an invisible sedative. I swept the powder into a cone made from the doctor's own letter of instruction and folded it shut, biding my time until tomorrow evening, when I could be certain of an audience without interruption.

***

'Come in, young man, come in. Very good... very good.' Dr. Amari was in his bed, robed in yellow silks embroidered with fantastical, paradisical birds. The room was boiling and thick as soup with the smell of cinnamon. Mrs. Waldrop had been correct. It smelt like decaying treasure, and I was sick of it. The whir of tiny gyres and the puff of tiny bellows increased in volume as I made for the teapot. 'How are you, Dr. Amari?' I asked, pouring myself a syrupy cup. Perhaps it was not the fineness of the china, but the thickness of the tea with suspension of cinnamon, that facilitated the shadow-puppetry at which I had once marvelled. 'Better, in advance, for your conversation' he said. With my back to the bed, I poured the doctor's brew, deliberately upending a measure of somniferous powder from the paper in my palm. I watched his curled talons navigate the swan's neck handle of the fine china, hold aside the tube of his golden respirator, and finally bring the teacup to his desert lips. For someone as infirm as the doctor, I thought, the narcotic should begin to take effect near-instantaneously. We waited in pleasant calm, insofar as such a thing could be achieved in those increasingly infernal chambers. The droning of machinery, the redolence of spice as if from great sacerdotal censers and even the oppressive warmth all conspired against my psychic tranquillity. I could not tarry any longer. 'Dr Amari', I began with studied goodness, 'will you be needing me to collect your cinnamon from the docks tomorrow?'

The doctor's eyes swam behind eyeglasses like aquaria. 'Yes, yes, of course – it's Friday, isn't it? The spicers come in on a Friday, weather permitting, yes, I shall need you to collect it. Why?' 'I suppose I was just wondering what you needed so much cinnamon for, after all'. The doctor gave a dry and demented chuckle. The apparatus at his chest was throbbing faster than usual. 'The cinnamon, boy! Always about the cinnamon are we? Hah! Very well. This much I shall tell you'. I waited for another excruciating span while the doctor's apparatus thundered. 'In his *Histories*, Herodotus describes two very unique creatures – two very rare birds, dwelling in distant Arabia. The first was said to make a journey to the Temple of the Sun in Egypt every five hundred years, bearing the body of its father in an egg made of spice. The second was said to build great nests exclusively from *Cinnamomum* – yes, boy, from cinnamon, the same stuff that's in our tea. The thing that I discovered before I came to this city – the thing that made it necessary to *escape to this country* in the first place, and to lie low forever in some obscure rooming-house – was that these two birds were not only existent, but were, in truth, one and the same species'.

I was beginning to fear that the man at the opium-house had slipped me rather too potent a strain of the poppy, or that misjudging the doctor's tolerance, I had accidentally sent him into narcotic delirium. The moment he regained his faculties, the old man continued his dazzling chain of non-sequiturs. 'The cinnamon is the vital catalyst of the bird's life-cycle. Cinnamon forms its nest and its tomb – and here is the important part. They are *exactly the same structure.* Here we have the oldest answer – a functioning model for true cosmic *ekpyrōsis.* The bird takes its father to the Temple of the Sun not for interment but for *rebirth*; rebirth in a ball of solar flame. The cinnamon is the essential agent – and this bird, of course, is the *phoenix'*.

And on this subject Dr. Amari would tell me no more, for the poppy had sent him to sleep.

I cursed under my breath. I was hoping it would merely loosen the old man's lips – but perhaps this was a blessing in disguise. I knelt to pick up the book by his bedside: a fine volume, with unmarked spine and cover. I thumbed it open to the frontispiece and stopped in my tracks. It was an issue of the London Mythophysical Society Journal. I turned to the contents, skimming the list of contributors: Prosper Harkness on the genesis of the jaw, Emmeline of Berkendorf on the ubiquity of the bush-spirit, and *there*, just as I thought – was Hassan Amari, 'Notes Towards Ekpyrōsis'. This book might be of great use, and if not, would surely fetch a pretty penny. Either way, it would leave with me. The doctor dozed in the nest of his great four-poster, tinny snores from his nosepiece accenting the syncopations of his apparatus. I followed the serpentine tangle of pipes and conduits down the bedside and across the floor. Perhaps it was finally time to see what the doctor kept sequestered in that oh-so-private antechamber. I parted the curtains of heavy brocade – there were two sets, bizarrely, one layered on top of the other – and immediately understood why. The smell of cinnamon was so intense here, so obscenely concentrated that I could taste it in my lungs. It burnt like the fumigating thuribles of Pandaemonium, with which the small room also shared an ambient temperature. In fact, I realised, this tiny space was more than likely the source of the apartment's wilting heat, not to mention the intoxicating fragrance of the entire boarding-house. The antechamber was poorly lit, its atmosphere opaque with ochre, but I could distinctly make out the great palisade of flattened gunny-sacks that insulated its perimeter, piled up like the cut purses of mermaids after an ebbtide of tainted wine. There were hundreds of them – thousands. But that was not the principal object of my amazement.

In the middle of it all stood a contraption which exceeded all schematic definition. When I say it looked byzantine, I imply that it might truly have been excavated from the ruins of Byzantium, where its primary function was the calcination of infidels. At its core was a spherical chamber of adamant, forty times the size of the largest cannonball. A sealed access-hatch of lead was set into its flank, and a ludicrous funnel protruded from the opposite side as if outlawed from the brass orchestra of the damned. Pipes and tubes multiplied from its base like paladin worms, the largest of which connected to a large canister, itself a heart of many arteries, above which great turbines slowly rotated to their rest. The turbines led onto another tangle of machinery – a tangle, I now believe, consisting largely of electromagnetic generators – before finally sprouting into that great umbilical cord that powered Dr. Amari's murmuring apparatus. The machine appeared dormant – before a muffled blast resounded from the central chamber. I stepped back. The metal orb was glowing with heat! Heat which was conducted to the canister – vaporising a liquid – turning the turbines – working the generators – sending energy down to the sleeping doctor. I heard the drip of liquid recondensing as the device dispersed heat from a radiating array. What nightmare engine had the doctor constructed? What alien intelligence could have marshalled thus the black metallurgies of the nether-hells? I moved closer to the machine. Beneath the access-hatch was a small plaque – engraved in lead, enamelled with gold. I squinted my eyes to read the inscription. *Eremiel.* There was nothing else for it. Protecting my hands with a pair of discarded cinnamon-bags, I began to twist open the hatch. I had to see – I had to know! I twisted and twisted, fearing that the machine would erupt into life again any moment and melt the flesh from my fingers – when the hatch opened.

A great drift of burnt cinnamon poured from the vessel, as sweet and bitter and suffocating as a pyroclastic flow of chai. The horrendous mixture spilled all over the floor, all over my hobnail boots, and from the gaping hatch an acrid spice-mist rouged the air as blood rouges water. I staggered back, one hand over my nose and mouth, the other waving at the vile fumes – when I heard a clattering from the vessel. There came a shuffling and a sifting as more charred cinnamon spilled from its yawning throat... and then a hoarse shriek, as something *emerged*.

I tumbled backwards through the curtains, throwing up great clouds of asphyxiating spice – and the thing followed me, shrieking like a phantom, stirring cyclones of cinnamon from ragged wings. Now it was in the doctor's apartment, shaking torrents of dust from its feathers, staining the silks, ripping at fine draperies as it scrabbled to escape. Now it was here – now it was there. Now it was up – now it was down. It was the creature that had choked to death a hundred thousand times since first it was sealed in that mad crypt of cinnamon. It was the creature condemned to perpetual rebirth so that an old philosopher could harness the fires of its resurrection; stealing its immortality in the quest to understand how. It was an engine for everlasting motion. It was the oldest answer. It was Dr. Amari's phoenix – it was Eremiel.

I had to stop it. The squawking was loud enough to wake the dead – loud enough to reveal my treachery! I leapt about trying to smite the creature from the sky; each time it retreated into the cavernous voids of the ceiling, screaming, raining ash and bituminous powder. It perched on a burgundy bedpost – I swung at it – and the creature took to the air again with a clatter of claws, ripping off the silken canopy. Its wingbeats upturned the three-legged tea table, shattering the crystal teapot. I swore. It screeched. It stooped at me with a flurry of wings, serrated beak snapping, flaring a vibrant crest; I tried to grapple it out of the air but it disentangled itself and careened straight through Dr. Amari's crystal chandelier. I stooped for a projectile, my hand closing around the Society journal – and lobbed it at the errant phoenix. It connected with scarcely a flutter of pages and a heavy thump, clubbing the bird beneath the wing and sending it to ground with a sickening crash. It scrabbled and screamed, rending the fine Persian rug to flinders – until I strode over and wrung its wretched neck.

Silence. I waited for a few minutes, ears hypersensitive to the sound of footsteps on the stairs – and nobody came. A wave of relief washed over me – when I realised what I had just heard. Silence. For the first time, I heard true silence in that apartment. I slowly turned my head to the disarrayed four-poster. Still nothing. Dr. Amari's apparatus has stopped working. Devoid of their supernatural battery, his tiny motors had ceased their vital contractions, his bellows their respiration – and the doctor had died in his sleep. Dr. Amari was dead, and, laying there in a chaos of rare silks and spiced natron, looked just like he had been dead for fifty years. But no such details troubled my thoughts. One word and one word only echoed through my mind – and it was *murder*. I looked down at the body of Eremiel – and gasped in astonishment. For on the Persian rug was no carcass at all – but only a small, cold, speckled egg.

Murder? Manslaughter perhaps – no, theft – no, nonsense, nothing of the sort, nothing at all! In that moment I realised that the death of Dr. Amari was the last downwards turn my life would ever take. It was all up from here. Here was my ticket, my escape from the entropy of everyday existence! I ran to the writing desk and swept the manuscript pages for the *Book of Eremiel* into the journal with which I had slain him. I would publish the book myself; earn a fortune and a place on the prestigious high table of the London Mythophysical Society. With the proverbial golden egg in my clutches, I had all the evidence I could ever need. When the time was right, I could build a nest of cinnamon just like the doctor had done, and *voila* – I had the blueprints for a perpetual motion machine, cosmic origins be blasted! The potential was limitless – but only if I could avoid all implication. I rummaged around the shelves until I found the doctor's address book, rifling through and tearing out the most promising page: 'L.M.S'. When the time came, I would need a way to contact the Society. I cushioned the phoenix egg with a silk handkerchief and left the doctor's chambers – only doubling back to collect my forgotten jacket. It was not my custom to visit so late in the evening, I had told nobody of my whereabouts, and I met nobody on the way down. This was perfect. Re-entering my room, I stashed the egg in the cupboard – far away, I made sure, from any culinary cinnamon – and began to sift through the stolen manuscript. I even drafted some letters to the London Mythophysical Society explaining my breakthrough. The death of Dr. Amari was as weightless as a feather on my soul – and what great fortune! Tomorrow was the day of the cinnamon shipment. I would discover the body first, and I would have a functional alibi. But everything would have to unfold as normal – no hitches, no aberrations. To that effect, I brewed myself a cup of tea from the last of the poppyseed powder, toasted the miserable dead old doctor, and dreamt.

The morning seemed to be going smoothly enough. The spice clipper – which, I noticed with satisfaction, happened to the same *Fenghuang* of my earliest fortunes – was some hours late in arrival, but this was relatively usual. Commerce, I thought, empire – this too was ekpyrotic, always rising, always falling. In the time I would ordinarily have consumed with malingering, I posted messages to the addresses of the L.M.S, announcing my breakthrough answer for the problem of a self-renewing universe, and promising a manuscript for review – hoping that one letter, at least, would find harbour. I picked up the shipment of cinnamon for Dr Amari, and as I began to walk back to the rooming house, I could have sworn I saw Lady Mei twirling her ivory hairpin at me from the window of the opium den. This troubled me little. I had seen substantially more distressing sights through that particular window. Dare I say it was proving quite a pleasant morning – until, that is, I returned to my lodgings.

Mrs. Waldrop was in tears. The moment she heard me set foot in the foyer, she ran downstairs. A limp handkerchief was flopping from her sleeve. 'Oh mister, don't go up to the doctor, mister, don't go up, there's been a terrible accident, a terrible, terrible accident…' I had spent so much of my life pretending there was a purpose, a progression, a rhythm to it all that I had gotten rather good at pretending. 'An accident?' I asked, 'what sort of-' 'He's dead, mister – Dr. Amari is dead! The poor, good old man! I shall have to sell the house – but what of that!' She began to weep harder, and I put down the cinnamon to embrace her. 'There, there', I said, smiling over her shoulder. 'He was old'. 'He was very old, that he was' said Mrs Waldrop, sniffing. 'I knew something was wrong the moment I woke up. The cinnamon – I couldn't smell the cinnamon…' My face turned pale – 'did you notice that, mister? Or maybe – maybe it was only after you left, that he… that he…' and she began to cry again. I consoled her as if from the blurb of an etiquette book, but the landlady was far too distraught to notice. She pulled away, sniffling. 'Here, mister, I've made you breakfast – like I would have made… for him. I wanted to thank you for… for… being his friend near the end of it all, always going up for tea… he was a lonely man, mister… you brought him such comfort, such joy', she sniffed, 'meeting you, it was like he'd been born all over again. But here, on the table, sorry if it's a bit cold – we'll wait for the inquest. I went in your larder for some of it – I hope that's alright'.

\*\*\*

Here I must put down my pen. I am out of money, out of tobacco – and worse, out of time. Two very suspicious looking gentlemen are talking to the chophouse keeper – and he's looking my way. The London Mythophysical Society did not take very kindly to the loss of one of their most senior contributors. My vainglorious communications could not be retracted. Soon the great downswing shall fall, and I shall know what drones the immortals pipe in hell, what rhythms in heaven. I dedicate these papers to the London Mythophysical Society. I have been wholly honest in their construction. When you read this, accept me for these words – for all these old answers to the most recent question of Dr. Amari's demise. Because all the evidence that remained for my breakthrough was the body of the man I had murdered for it. And despite the landlady's fears, the egg which glistened on the plate that fateful morning was far from cold. Its orange yolk burned with the infinite radiance and fury of the sun.

# NAOMI

'You know, if you put that thing on, I have a strange feeling you'll probably lose your mind'. Naomi swore at me with her eyes. Nobody else could curse so eloquently without saying a single word. Any rejoinder which my feeble wits might conceive in the moment would be immediately caught in that parrying-dagger gaze of hers and twisted quite out of hand. It would be as though a swordsman of the high Renaissance had challenged a mime to single combat and suffered first blood from a distance of twenty strides at the point of no weapon at all – and I'm pretty much convinced that this precise experience is the unique property of love. 'You have about forty-five minutes', she replied, 'until you lose yours'. I attempt a playful objection, since non-confrontational confrontation is my natural mode of address. '*Find* it, more like'. 'Trust me. You know they used to call *Psilocybe aztecorum* 'The Flesh of the Gods'. You'll find a mind, I'm sure, hell, maybe even more than one – but it probably won't belong to you'. 'Yeah yeah'. 'Won't be mine either'. 'Good to know. But honestly Naomi that thing looks horrific. If I were you – I wouldn't play around with it'. 'Like this?' 'Almost exactly like that'.

I'm afraid to say that this sort of thing always happens to us, although I'd be lying if I didn't also mention the fact that we persistently sought it out. This would probably be our last long summer together before the rodent-race, and we'd both be damned if we didn't spend it going out in a blaze of heroic immaturity. And that largely involved a healthy dose of ethnobotanical experimentation, sunburn and staring into rockpools – all in an effort to prime our minds for the influence of the outré, of the utterly weird. Naomi had an uncanny knack for finding it. Among the beachglass and cowrie shells and hagstones and salvaged sinkers that jangled at her neck like surf against shingle was a tiny driftwood dowsing rod, which I've always found attractively overdetermined. Anyway. Just last week we had knocked on the door of one of those quaint little curiosity shops endemic to seaside towns; the kinds with balding old rocking-horses stabled in the window beside galleon preserves and amateur sack-of-sawdust seagull taxidermies almost as manky as the living articles. The first weird thing was that it opened. For a long time I had been under the impression that shops like this one, apparently designed (with some forethought) to *repel* potential customers, covered their overhead exclusively with caches of pirate treasure turned up from beneath the floorboards a day before it was due every month. But the door opened, the elderly proprietress had welcomed us in with a shuffle of her carpet slippers, and five minutes later Naomi was holding a decorated conch which had served as the head of a ceremonial mace belonging to the chief priest of some ancient South Seas Island kingdom. 'If you put it to your ear', the old woman had said, 'you can hear the ancestors whispering their blessings'. I put the shell to my ear. And while my neurotransmitters were unquestionably still scrambled by the overrunning 'question and answer' segment of whatever cerebral symposium had most recently attended me; I am beyond certain that, whatever was being whispered in those ivory depths, 'blessings' was a very generous interpretation. Naomi wouldn't tell me what she heard, though disturbingly enough it seemed to please her. And although I could reliably recognise insults and imprecations (indeed curses tend to be the first words one acquires in the study of a new language) I am still not fluent in her native dialect of gazes and glances and glares…

Naomi usually considered it unfair to search after strange things in the shelves of Leaf's lighthouse – 'it's just too easy', she'd complain. But for whatever reason that's exactly where the day had taken us. Leaf lived alone in a tiny, decommissioned lighthouse which tottered at the end of the spit like a rook in the headlights of a rampaging queen. It was the only building I had ever laid eyes upon which simultaneously conveyed the impressions of towering *and* cowering, a quality which it shared with its slightly deranged and hermitical habitant, who was both as tall as his tales were and nearly as short of sense. Painted in swirling sunset colours on a broken surfboard over the doorframe was the phrase 'somebody's home, but the lights are off'. There was also no door to speak of. Only a cascading curtain of frayed nylon rope and tangled line and scavenged shoelace strung with beads and shells and bottlecaps beachcombed over a hundred idle hours. Leaf firmly believed that the beach hut (his previous residence) had only washed away because it was equipped with a traditional door. You couldn't blame a tempest for the power of its knock. Makeshift windchimes hung from the many driftwood structures which, depending on one's angle of approach and the position of the sun, might correctly have been identified as enthusiastic attempts at bohemian sculpture, experimental furniture, altars to short-sighted or at least very charitable spirits, or flotsam tossed from distant wrecks. Inside, the lighthouse was not much different. Wherever they were not completely overgrown with creaking shelves, the walls were stacked and hung with a thousand material obscurities which Leaf had either found on the beach, collected on his youthful travels as some sort of marine zoologist, or dreamt up during his all too frequent trips to places omitted from the atlas by earthly cartographers. When, on rare occasions, the social instinct predominated in his rather erratic character, Leaf would attempt to peddle these artefacts to passers-by, sweetening the deal with outrageous stories and usually accepting the same currency. And on the remote spit which high tide was known to cut off from the mainland, 'passers-by' meant the rare inquisitive tourist, Naomi, and myself. That summer we must have visited often enough to earn special privileges: anything and everything was ours for the taking. I must say that I had to agree with Naomi's statement that seeking the fantastical in such a place was slightly unfair, though it certainly wouldn't stop me. 'Anything' and 'everything' that found its home in Leaf's collection did so on account of its utter estrangement from the canons of normality. If any given item had something so quotidian as a story, one would be inclined to bet one's bottom dollar on its fictitiousness if only for the satisfaction of losing nearly every time.

It was right in the midst of our conversation that Leaf himself stumbled down the spiral stairs. He looked, as he always did, as though some seafaring man had decided to pack a hippie in a barrel of salt so that the 'good vibes' wouldn't spoil over the course of a long voyage. His long hair looked like Irish moss that had crisped and bleached in the sun by the water's edge. He had a tattoo of an omniscient eye on the back of his right hand but kept it covered up because it wouldn't stop winking at him. Like many who had spent their best years chasing the iridescent dragon through counterculture's prehistoric marshes, he had actually taken enough, and for long enough, to catch it. He had spent the next chapter of his life gradually clambering from its tail to its head: and upon finding that it came to a perfect loop, came full circle himself. In short, Leaf was the twitchiest, most paranoid and by far the most paradoxical old beach-cryptid in existence. In his solitary, shoreline shrine to strangeness, he was himself the crown jewel. Once he told us that a bit of him had dissolved from looking too long into the sea, and that's why he was the way he was. We both knew it took sterner stuff to dissolve a human mind, and to put it bluntly, that such stuff had been took – and weren't at all sure whether the statement had been intended for a metaphor. Sadly, it probably hadn't been. I had received much the same impression when Leaf took me aside and, eyes darting nervously as if in anticipation of an intruder, solemnly confided that he had been struck by lightning eighteen times and knew it would happen again. Not even Naomi could unriddle that one. Anyway. I was his friend, and I think he was mine, and the crazy old fellow seemed to remember this arrangement after only a few moments of flabbergasted terror at our presence by the foot of the lighthouse stairs. He looked at the pleading expression on my face, then looked at Naomi holding the – well, the object. The pupils of his pale eyes were always randomly contracting and dilating, as if the focusing mechanism had finally frazzled as a result of overexposure to visions it was not designed to accommodate. They lighted at last on the object that was the locus of our quarrel. 'Oh', he mumbled, half to himself and half to the faeries, 'that old thing. I wouldn't put that on if I were you. You'll probably lose your mind'.

A smile flashed over my face. For a life lived, like mine, between the back foot and the wrong side of the bed, moments like this were worth relishing. Of course, Naomi knew to restrain her standoffish tendencies to deprive me of any surplus emotional satisfaction – which is fair play, as far as I'm concerned. She was the finest sparring partner I'd ever fallen for, and however much I found myself desiring to the contrary in the small and desperate hours of morning, losing to her felt just as good as winning. And as much as the coincidence of Leaf's alliance in the matter of the sinister artefact suggested some ultimate and inscrutable truth resonating across the cosmic lattice – I didn't parade this little triumph. To maximise pleasure, which is scarce enough as is, I'd always settle for both. Snatching defeat from the jaws of victory.

'Leaf', she began, ignoring me, 'what are you talking about. And more to the point – what *is* this thing?'. Leaf looked at Naomi as if she was herself a rather peculiar specimen. And then, as if addressing a neighbour who had contradicted his assessment of the day's weather on account of some private report from the meteorological office of her gammy knee, answered with mildly affronted insouciance – 'why, it's my whale-louse tiara'.

The object was somewhere in between avant-garde accessory and extraterrestrial lifeform. It was relatively large and crustaceous in appearance, with a pale segmented body which bore distressing resemblance to a flattened length of human spine. It had six pairs of legs, wickedly hooked and plated with chitin. Of these pairs, the lowermost three were closely grouped, tremendously hypertrophied and inwardly curled to form a closed ring whose circumference was uncannily identical to that of Naomi's head. The central, vertebral mass of the object was also curved inwards, on a vertical rather than a horizontal axis, so that it would lie flush to the dome of its wearer's scalp. The other appendages (of which the uppermost were equipped with formidable pincers) were arrayed in such a manner as to give the whole assemblage a loose, basket-like frame. Yet the vertex was perhaps its most disturbing component. The tiara had a tiny head, which, if worn, would rest right at base of the wearer's skull. And while it was amply equipped with an arsenal of palps, mandibles and forcipules, black compound eyes of mineral simplicity and the osseous knuckles of horn-like feelers – there was something distinctly characterful about its organisation, something suggestively anthropoidal in the tessellation of its chitinous plates – something almost human. The effect was rather like one of those startling instances of Batesian mimesis, where the staring eyes of some great nocturnal predator turn out to be painted onto the wings of an enormous dusky moth.

'Is it real?' Leaf's eyebrows knitted together with genuine concern. 'I've never seen anything that wasn't at least a little bit real'. 'Where did you find it?', I ventured the question before Naomi could get 'more to the point' again. This was a distressing habit of hers. The old man's brows were now veritably crocheted with effort – possibly mnemonic, possibly creative. 'It was left me by a lover', he suddenly said, 'lost at sea. Her body was never found, yes, lost at sea, lost at sea. I remember'. True or not, this was a startling tenor for the Leaf-lore to take. 'We're sorry to hear that'. 'No, don't be. I seem to recall it was best for us both. Let me tell you about whale-lice. Commensalism was her speciality. We were studying marine invertebrates – yes, *Cyamidae,* or whale-lice as they're known: not true lice, not parasitic, strictly speaking, not mutualistic either. What was I saying? Oh yes. She disappeared without a trace'. Naomi was scrutinising the tiara as she spoke. 'And about the whale-lice, Leaf?' 'Well, one thing I find unendingly fascinating about whale-lice is that every species of cetacean – and indeed every population within a single cetacean species – has its own unique symbiont species. A bottlenose, for instance, is far less craggy and cumbersome than a humpback – and so their whale-lice get flatter and smoother with stronger legs and larger claws. The movement and migration of an individual whale is the whale-louse version of our continental drift; sometimes the landmasses clash, populations cross over and lose their identities, but most of the time it's a million

whale-louse-years of speciating solitude at a stretch'.
'Fascinating indeed'. 'And how does this relate to...
this 'tiara', as you call it?' 'Oh, well, that's the part of
the story I can't remember'. 'I'm pretty sure you can'.
'Why yes, now that you mention it, I believe I can. It
was on one of Sara's last research trips that they
discovered the mermaid. A carcass, of course, long-
dead and bloated, adrift near the surface. Well, she
must have been drifting for a terribly long time, or
else must have been particularly repulsive to the
usual scavengers – because this mermaid's corpse
had somehow acquired its own population of whale-
lice. And what's more, she had sustained them for
sufficient generations for the population to
specialise. What you're holding is a whale-louse
adapted to the humanoid, rather than to the
cetacean, anatomy. That one was found on her head'.

At this point I was beginning to feel
pleasantly suggestible, although I tried not to blink
for too long lest my imagination seize the
opportunity of a blank canvas and run away with me.
'It does look for all the world like some terrible
eldritch crown, doesn't it? Hey, Naomi, have you
read *The Shadow over Innsmouth*? There's this
brilliant scene at the start with a truly bizarre tiara,
engraved with-' 'No, I'm afraid I couldn't suffer
through the opening exposition. Leaf, I have to say
that's a brilliant tale and I wish it were mine. But I

really don't understand why putting this thing on, bizarre as it is, would make me lose my sanity'. The old man blinked, suddenly furtive, unsure of himself – which was exactly the typical effect Naomi had on people. 'Well, err, you know how it is with mermaids… they don't always follow scientifical expectations. I just have a very strong feeling that sort of thing would happen. Oh, and, err – perhaps I should have mentioned this earlier – notice how firmly it holds its shape? It's not like the jangly old shrimp you find washed up in the surf. In other words… I'm pretty sure it's still alive'. Naomi looked Leaf as directly as possible in his oscillating eyeballs. I watched her deft and capable hands. The calcified coronet didn't so much as tremble in their grip. 'It's dry as bone', she said bone-dryly. 'Dormant, perhaps', said Leaf, beginning to quaver. How could she be so bloody *certain* about everything? And how could that be as comforting as it was discomforting? 'I still don't think you should put it on', I attempted, 'let's just find something else – or let's go. You have a wonderful mind, and it would be a shame to lose it. And besides, I think I'll need a companion very soon – the saner the better'. And now Naomi turned to transfix me with that brilliant linguistic stare of hers. 'You know, I'm slightly tired of playing the trip-sitter. So what if I 'lose my mind', as you insist on calling it? If there's one thing I've figured out about myself this summer it's that the blasted thing wants out. Everything I do is just another excuse to lose myself completely. And what? I don't see the problem with that – and I don't think you do either'. I was utterly confounded. 'Jeez Naomi, that's dramatic. I'm sorry – but please, don't put it on'. 'You know', she said, 'I hate to say it, I really do, but somehow I think you'd love me more if I wasn't around'. In one motion, the whale-louse tiara was on her head. Did it move slightly? I'm not sure. It fit her perfectly. And then she disappeared. The tiara clattered to the floor. 'Oh dear', said Leaf in a mounting panic, 'oh dear oh dear oh dear' – and then the mushrooms well and truly hit.

Leaf was hopping up and down in nervous shock. I must have produced some inquisitive noise, though I couldn't be sure – *Psilocybe aztecorum* was coming on so strongly that the orchestra of waves gathering thousands of miles offshore was synchronising with the ebb and flow of reality whose subscription to Newtonian physics had ended sixty seconds ago. I was dimly aware of Leaf mumbling about how the body was only the outermost layer of the mind, or perhaps the thought had germinated naturally in my own body-mind matrix, but all I knew for certain is that Naomi was gone and I had to get somewhere safe and quiet to ride out the impromptu hyperspace initiation. I stumbled outside through the kelp of curtain into a storm of stimulus. Breakers were roving over the ocean in every direction at once. The clouds – usually my favourite things to study in such situations, on account of their infinitesimal shifting and swirling – were mauve and pregnant with a brood of thunders. Very shortly after the dedication of my young life to the pursuit of the unfathomable, I had the good fortune to see in exhibition the fossil of a pregnant plesiosaur, the bones of whose unborn child were distinctly visible in the calcareous cage of its own. Now imagine an endless recursion of plesiosaurs pregnant with pregnant plesiosaurs, displayed with X-ray starkness, and each flash of the radiographer's device was the conception of a tadpole thunderbolt; and was it not also true that the instantaneous release of zinc that marked the meeting of sperm and egg cells caused a microscopic firework of photons? How strange and how wonderful that my whole being was at one point expressed in a language of pure light. And this language far antedated the chemical matter of my conception. For in that moment I was secure in the knowledge that all my potential self was curled up in the first spark of affection that flashed in the eye of my earliest ancestor. I had travelled down the line of inheritance in a fuse of flashing eyes which exploded into new life with every generation until I manifested. Naomi had the most communicative eyes I had ever known, but if they had ever glimmered in the morse of tomorrow's ancestors I probably hadn't been paying attention. And by the way – the clouds looked something like that.

It was only when I somehow realised that the rising tide had cut the lighthouse off from the mainland that it struck me how incredibly bad the timing of all this was. That's what happens when you live spontaneously, I thought with my last rations of clarity – you tend to combust. If I hadn't wasted my last lucidity on bad *bon mots*, I probably would have made the connection with Naomi's quite unexpected disappearance at the claws of the whale-louse tiara, but given the present circumstances the whole situation no longer struck me as particularly extraordinary. That was the rather counterintuitive effect of consciousness-contorting substances on seekers after strangeness: for as long as they lasted, one was essentially immune to surprise. But unfortunately for me, the daydream equivalent of existential nightmare was still very much on the table. Leaf's driftwood sculptures were waving at me with innumerable antennae, swaying through the aether like great stick insects in rituals of courtship. The windchimes were tinkling in tongues. I staggered to the water's edge. Dark basaltic rock gave way to glittering sand. There was no chance of swimming back – indeed, I could barely walk – but what did it matter; I had foresworn my locomotive willpower the moment I had decided to lie down with my sandals in the seafoam. Normally I would have been deeply hesitant to roll my beloved Hawaiian-print robe in the sand. Naomi had made it for me, along with a pointy straw hat, as part of an alternative style she called 'beach wizard', which she definitely pulled off far better than I ever could. I think it was inspired by Leaf. Good lord. I was wearing her attempt at wearing him. And where was I amongst all this wearing? Lying on my back in the sand. Fitting, really. I closed my eyes. The fungal dimension was sepia-tinted, the colour of chitin, of red sediment and earthenware, because the eyes of the mind have some inscrutable sympathy with those of the flesh, and that was the colour of the sun through my closed eyelids. It occurred to me that I had a particular fondness for objects of this colour – old maps, sandstone monuments, strange bones, all tea-stain-yellow things of orders ancient and unknown; and perhaps that attraction arose from the primal desire to experience again the chromic pleasure of sun through skin. I was starting to hear things chirp and chitter without clear corporeal sources. I don't remember how much I had taken but Naomi's grandmother was a *curandera* and (let me tell you) this stuff she had gotten was certainly beginning to feel sacred. The chittering increased in intensity, or maybe it was only my fixation that did. I opened my eyes in wonder – and saw that the mysterious susurration was not entirely endogenous. For there, half-buried not twenty feet from where I lay, was the shipwrecked corpse of a plesiosaur. A whale. A juvenile humpback. At first I thought it was caked with sand, but somehow I managed to haul myself closer – closer and still closer, until I could smell the gunge of its rotting blubber, hear the creak of its ivory farthingales, and see the chittering mass of whale-lice overwhelming it like a second skin. Skeleton rust incarnadine. Sunset rose caliche. Endless tiny colours-voices-shapes. The satyr-chorus in a beautiful foreign play. 'Isn't it funny how decomposition obliquely fulfils the seven essential processes of life?', said the whale.

'What an interesting observation', I thought loudly in return. Even over the crispening and clicking and clattering of its crustaceous colonists, I knew the great whale could hear me. It wept gelatine from a lustreless dead eyeball the size of my fist. The great keel of its lower jaw, half-collapsed, was agape with urbane disbelief at having run aground. Waves brushed vainly against its ponderous displacement, a grieving mother dandling her foregone baby. 'I'll tell you something else', it continued, never moving its sunken mouth, 'when an organism's immune system is compromised, its microbiome goes haywire. Death is the ultimate compromise because it swings the locus of life to the symbionts'. 'Who are you?' my mind asked for me. The whale replied with pacific wisdom. 'I am Tlaloc, lord of water and of fructifying growth'. '…Awesome'. 'I'll tell you something else you might find interesting', said Tlaloc, 'if you'll follow me'. The world still warping around me, I put my hand to the flank of the carcass. Tiny whale-lice of translucent bronze began to crawl between my fingers. And then we merged.

Tlaloc swam serenely through the vastitude. I swam through him, enmeshed in the tranquil totality of his bodymind. 'Isn't it funny', he began in his familiar fungal idiom, 'how the development of a foetus in the womb restages the organism's evolutionary development in miniature? Humpback whales have baleen, and not teeth, yet our unborn children spend a portion of their pre-natal existence growing and re-absorbing their teeth because we had them long ago in the Distant Time'. 'Wow'. 'Human foetuses have gills for the same reason'. 'You're so right', I murmured unquestioningly. 'Ontogeny recapitulates phylogeny'. Over the course of the conversation, I had become acutely conscious that my anthropoid form and faculties had been gradually dissolving, so that the memory of my being now took the form of a whale calf gestating in Tlaloc's metamorphic womb. 'What does that actually